HELD BY THE HIGHLANDER

A Scottish Time Travel Romance

BLANCHE DABNEY

CONTENTS

Contact Blanche Dabney

Newsletter - blanchedabney.com/sign-up/

Instagram - instagram.com/blanchedabney

Chapter One

It felt as if they'd gone back in time.

"He was born right here," Janet said, pointing at the bed. "Isn't it incredible? The old hall of the MacIntyres. Eight hundred years and just a few inches between us and the most famous laird of the clan. Andrew MacIntyre's actual bedroom. I can't believe I'm finally here."

Beth glanced down at the guidebook again. She was ashamed to admit she knew almost nothing about the MacIntyre clan but then the most avid scholar would be put to shame compared to her mother. Janet Dagless had been obsessed with the MacIntyres ever since she found out that Andrew had married a Dagless all those years ago.

"They were the largest of the highland clans," Janet said, seeing Beth's nose in the guidebook. "Did you know that? They had a lineage that went back way before the Norman invasion. Andrew was the last laird to be born here in the old hall. After his birth, they built a castle that still houses his descendants today."

The castle was next on their list of places to visit. They were going to see if they could find any evidence of the Dagless family name in the archives of the clan library, if they ever got away from the old hall.

Janet continued, "We might actually be related to him? Distantly, of course, but still, imagine that. There might be a tiny bit of highland blood in both of us." She stared again at the old bed. "Andrew was actually born right here. Amazing. What are you looking at?"

Beth realized her mind had wandered. She had been distracted by the ceiling. "It's stone vaulted," she explained. "Exactly how I'd have built it if I'd been around back then."

"So what if it's vaulted?"

"So it's a domestic building. Not many could afford to vault them in stone. Must have cost a fortune. Good idea though. That way it'd be protected if there was a fire."

"You and your architecture again. Your ancestor was born right here and all you care about is what the ceiling's made out of."

"We don't know if we're related to him yet, Mom."

"Come on. How common is our surname? I bet we are. I wonder if the current laird would be willing to do a DNA test. Maybe we could ask him?"

"I doubt it."

Janet looked at her daughter. "What if he's single? I could hook you up with him."

"How would that work if we're related?"

"I thought you didn't believe we were."

"It's academic anyway, mom. I told you, I don't want to get married."

"And I told you I don't believe you. Every girl wants to get married."

"Not me. I'm happy being single."

"Nonsense." Janet sniffed loudly. "I can smell burning. Can you smell burning?"

Beth's nose wrinkled. "Actually, I think I can."

She turned to the bedroom door and was about to open it when her mother grabbed her hand. "Look, down there."

From the gap under the door wisps of black smoke were drifting in, thin tendrils that slowly rose toward them as if trying to grab hold of them by the ankles. "Don't open it, Beth."

She crossed to the window only to find it was bolted shut.

"Can you break it?" Janet asked, grabbing hold of the locket around her neck, the same thing she did every time something worried her. On the day she'd been diagnosed, she didn't once let go of the locket.

Beth examined the window. "It's safety glass. Must be to stop anyone breaking in."

"But we need to break out. It's getting worse, Beth. What do we do?"

I don't know, she thought, looking anxiously at the smoke as it began to fill the room.

It was supposed to be a relaxing trip to Scotland together. It was meant to help her mother get away from the endless hospital visits, forget about the diagnosis for a little while.

Beth booked the trip and only revealed the surprise when it was all paid for. That way all her mom had to do was enjoy it, not worry about how to pay for it. She drove them hundreds of miles north to MacIntyre Hall. She paid for the tickets, bought the guidebook, tried to learn a bit about the MacIntyres as they walked around, tried not to think how frail her mom looked.

"Move back, mom," she said, crossing the room once again. "I'm going to look out there."

"Wait," Janet began but it was too late. Beth turned the handle and as the door opened a wall of flame blew inward, engulfing the pair of them.

Beth felt no pain. She always remembered that afterward. Her lungs should have filled with acrid black smoke as the roaring fire surrounded her but she was left strangely untouched by it. Not even a hint of heat. No sensation at all.

The flames licked past her, swallowing up the centuries old bedframe, running straight up the dark wood panels on the wall, racing across the ceiling but still shying away from her as if afraid to touch her.

She looked back, groping for her mother's outstretched hand, seeing it for the briefest of moments before it vanished from sight in the thick black smoke. "Mom," she cried out but there was no answer beyond the roar of the flames.

She couldn't move. She was too scared. Then there was a blast of wind from behind her. Had Mom somehow managed to get the window open after all?

The wind grew stronger and yet it had no effect on the flames or the smoke. All it did was push her forward through the inferno to the corridor outside the laird's bedroom.

She was buffeted across the floor, her feet sliding just above the melting carpet. Around her the flames moved aside as if directed by an unseen force. She called out as she was propelled forward. "This way, Mom. Follow me."

She groped behind her and managed to catch hold of something. She tried to look back but the wind grew stronger, a hurricane blast that sent her hurtling along the corridor to the door at the end which swung open as she approached.

She burst into the open, falling to the ground, coughing and spluttering, fighting to get fresh air into her lungs as the smoke swirled like a tornado around her.

The gale died away as quickly as it had come, leaving her in a daze. She looked back at the burning hall, little more now than a wall of flames. The few parts still standing were crumbling before her eyes.

There would be nothing left when it was over, just a piece of scorched earth to show where Andrew MacIntyre was born.

She was still holding something. She looked at her hand. Her fingers were wrapped around a length of wood, the end on fire. How had she got hold of that? She dropped it to the ground and looked around for her mother.

She felt completely disorientated. She glanced around her, taking less than a second to work out something was very wrong. There were no familiar landmarks around her. She thought she'd come back out the way they'd gone in but she must have got confused. There was no parking lot next to her, no gift shop, no tourists anywhere to be seen other than a couple over by the woods who appeared to be arguing about something. Between them and her were only but green fields divided into strips, the stalks of wheat rippling as if in a light breeze, completely unaffected by the hurricane that had just blown her off her feet.

Beyond the fields and trees jagged mountains rose toward the sky, their peaks covered with snow.

Where was her mother?

"Mom," she screamed, running toward the hall. "Mom!"

The intense heat stopped her, pushing her back. Shielding her face, she screamed again. "Mom!"

There was a thundering sound behind her and she turned in time to see men on horseback racing her way across the fields.

They were wearing perfect medieval costume. Tartan baldric over one shoulder in the bright red MacIntyre colors, brown or green hose covering their legs, swords that swung back and forth from each baldric as they slowed their horses.

One of the men was clearly in charge of the others. He leapt down and, ignoring her, directed his men, talking in a Scottish accent so broad she couldn't understand a word he was saying.

All of a sudden he ran straight into the flames. Beth only caught a glimpse of his stern face before he vanished.

He hadn't hesitated for a second, just sprinted into the inferno. Seconds later he came back out, an unconscious woman in his arms. Other tartan clad men followed him, darting into what was left of the hall. How were they not catching alight?

Beth had no idea how they were doing it. She tried twice to get in there but each time her skin began to singe and her body refused to let her get any closer. She could only watch as more people were dragged out, coughing and spluttering as they came, the remains of their clothes smoking.

She tried shouting again. "Mom, where are you?"

To her left people were throwing buckets of water onto the flames but she knew there was nothing anyone could do to save the place. Where were the fire engines? The hoses? The men in helmets and oxygen masks?

The building was gone. All that history, hundreds and hundreds of years, gone in moments. The stone vaulting had done nothing to protect it. Why not? It should have acted as a firebreak. Something had gone very wrong.

She kicked herself for even caring about that when her mother was still missing.

There was a noise to her right and she looked that way. Some men were running away from the hall toward an untidy row of thatched cottages. She frowned as she looked at them. Their tartan was blue, markedly different to the men who'd first appeared on horseback. Each of the blue group held a flaming torch much like the one on the grass beside her.

She couldn't remember seeing other medieval houses next to the hall when they arrived. Had she missed them? They were eerily accurate recreations of village hovels from the twelfth century. As she watched, the torches were pressed to their thatched roofs.

Instantly, the homes were ablaze. "No," she cried, unable to believe what she was seeing. Was it some kind of ultra-real re-enactment?

If so, things had definitely gone too far.

They had given her and her mother no warning of what was happening and surely it was dangerous to set fire to buildings with visitors still inside them?

The leader of the horseback riders emerged from the fire with another victim of the blaze in his arms. He quickly took in the scene.

The men who had been throwing water on the fire were running after the torch bearers, swords out ready. Villagers from the burning homes were trying to save what they could, throwing their possessions out onto the grass. Those rescued from the hall were slowly sitting up on the grass. Others were helping where they could, providing fresh water and blankets for the wounded.

His eyes took all that in and then he looked at her. "MacLeish," he snarled, his voice no more than a low growl.

Beth wanted to ask him if he'd seen her mother but she couldn't speak all of a sudden. His eyes were burning twin holes into her soul.

He was intimidating enough even if he hadn't looked so furious. A clear six foot five, he obviously took re-enactment seriously. There were taut muscles spread across his chest, his shoulders looking like they more used to carrying horses, than riding them. His skin was blackened by the smoke and soot, sweat pouring down him creating pathways through the soot.

He had dark hair that was closely cropped. His eyes were equally dark and as he continued to stare at her. He looked livid.

He knelt for long enough to lay the elderly woman in his arms out on the grass. Then he stood up again, grabbing Beth's tee-shirt in his enormous fist. "Why?" he said, his voice becoming a whisper and all the more aggressive for it. "Why would you burn Pluscarden?"

"I...I..." Beth stuttered. "I didn't. I'm not one of them, I swear."

He turned his head and she looked too. The escaping bunch had dropped their torches and were clambering onto horses. They began galloping away, firing arrows back at their pursuers as they went. One of the chasing men fell, an arrow in his chest.

The giant holding Beth bellowed at the top of his voice, "MacIntyres. To me."

The surviving men ran back to him at once, leaving the group on horseback to vanish into the distance.

In moments she was surrounded by men, all of them looking at the torch their leader was holding. He stared at her again.

One of them prodded her in the back. "You should have run with your kin when you had the chance, lassie. One of ours is dead. Perhaps we should redress the balance with your blood."

"Look at what you've done," their leader said, letting go of her top to grab her chin, forcing her to stare down at the victims on the ground. His hand squeezed tightly, making her gasp. "Was it worth whatever Duff paid you?"

Beth's heart began to pound with fear. He could pick me up and throw me like I'm a caber, she thought, fear growing inside her. Snap me in half without breaking a sweat.

"Okay, time out," she said as the other men pointed their swords at her, swords that looked a little bit too real for comfort. "This isn't funny anymore. I'm not part of your stupid re-enactment so stop acting like I am. I want my mom."

Chapter Two

"Just like a MacLeish," Andrew said. He looked at her fear filled face. "Tremble in my grasp but only because you're caught. Come onto my land, burn the homes of my people and then when captured red handed, you cry out for your mommy."

Fury washed over him but as he looked at her the anger vanished like the morning mist when the sun rose high in the sky. She looked terrified but all of a sudden he wanted to protect her, not hurt her. Why was that?

People had been burned alive. This was no time to pat her on the head and say there, there, never mind.

She squirmed and fought to free herself from his grip. He let go, momentarily confused by his own feelings. He couldn't stop staring at her.

She had eyes like none he'd ever seen before. Her hair was MacIntyre red and her eyes were ocean blue, staring back at him in terror.

She tried to run but his men stopped her at once. Her hair fell over her face as she twisted in place to try and escape.

What hair it was. Cascading around her shoulders, it framed her face perfectly. Even with soot smearing her features she looked beautiful.

For a moment he was speechless but then he recovered himself. She might be as attractive as a siren from the sea but that didn't change what she'd done with the help of her cowardly comrades.

Burned the hall where he'd been born. No doubt they'd thought he was in there when they set the blaze. Indeed, he was meant to be inside the hall that morning but at the last minute he'd been called away to the new castle and he'd only returned in time to find the place ablaze.

Innocent people had been murdered. Murder meant escalation to clan war, something he could have well done without. Winter was coming and the Normans were rumored to be heading north again.

"Do we kill her?" Finley asked, bringing him out of his thoughts. "Send her head back as a warning?"

"She comes with us," he replied. "Take hold but do not harm her. We may be able to use her to bargain with MacLeish. He's likely as not to value one of his own that looks as bonny as she."

She started to complain, talking about tickets and re-enactors and again calling out for her mommy amongst a load of other nonsense words he didn't understand.

"We cannae have her blathering all the way to the castle," Derek said, slapping her across the face. "Bind her legs and arms. Get a gag over her face."

"No," Andrew replied, angry at Derek's unnecessary violence. "We are MacIntyres, not MacLeishes. "We dinnae beat women."

"I say at least bind her," Derek replied, his voice showing no sign of contrition. "Unless you want her to escape?"

"That is not how you speak to your laird," Gillis said. "Apologize at once."

"I will not. He's clearly been bewitched by her already."

"How dare you suggest that your laird is so easily..."

Andrew raised his voice over their bickering. "Now is not the time for an argument. Derek, this isnae your decision. Gillis, I can fight my own battles. As for you, lassie, I apologise for that blow. If you will ride to yon castle without blather or violence, I willnae bind your limbs. What say you?"

She didn't move. "I want my mom."

"We'll get you to your ma soon enough. Now will you swear to-"

"You know where she is? You've seen her? Where is she?"

There was a cry of pain behind him. "Hold onto her a moment," he said to his men before turning away.

He knelt beside the moaning woman, taking a damp cloth from one of the villagers. "Be still, you'll be all right."

Derek tapped him on the shoulder. "We should not stay long. They will come back in greater numbers."

"You'd know," Wallace said. "Wouldn't you? They're your kin Derek MacLeish."

"So what if they come back?" Finley snapped at the same time. "Perhaps we'll have a straight fight for once."

Andrew spoke without getting up, still mopping the woman's' brow. "What good is it to leave our wounded to die just because you fancy a scrap? We can fight their whole army later. Right now, our people need our help."

He barely recognized the woman moaning in her sleep. Most of her skin was charred and acrid smelling. Her eyes remained closed as her moans subsided.

He looked up at Gillis. "Get as many carts as you can. Finley, you take a couple of men with you and gather horses. Help the villagers bring what they can and be along by nightfall. They will be safer inside castle walls than out here. I will have James prepare the infirmary for your return. The rest of you, spread the word. All are to come into the castle by the time the moon rises."

"My laird." The men got to work.

He frowned, looking down at the injured woman on the ground. "It's Mary, isn't it?"

The woman moaned in response, trying to speak.

"Save your strength. Help is coming." He stood up. "Make haste, Gillis before it is too late."

With that he marched over to his horse and leapt onto its back. The MacLeish woman was standing next to it, looking unsure of herself. He reached out a hand. "Come with me lassie."

"You'll take me to my mom?"

"Aye, I swear.

She nodded, accepting his outstretched hand. As their fingers touched he looked into her eyes, lost in that deep ocean once more. She looked away and only then did he come back to himself, lifting her effortlessly onto the horse.

He kicked the sides of the beast. Slowly, they began to trot out of the village.

He didn't look back. He didn't need to. What was left of the fire was already burning itself out. All that was left was for the ruins to crumble. He was already thinking about rebuilding.

The hall had stood fifty years, not bad considering it had a kitchen inside. Next time they would have the kitchen as a separate building like at the castle. That way when it burned as they all did sooner or later, the hall itself would be safe. If only there were a way to fireproof it better.

In many ways the MacLeishes had done him a favor. He had been thinking of rebuilding for some time but something else always came up. Finishing the castle took up so much of his time he had neglected the maintenance of the hall. It had been crumbling for years.

He really needed to hire a master mason, stop trying to do everything himself. But who could he trust to do it right?

All of the masons in the highlands were working for the MacLeishes on their new fangled hexagonal keep. It would cost a fortune to poach one from them and knowing old Duff, he'd probably interpret even that as motion to war.

He did not relish the idea of clan war at all. All he'd ever wanted was peace. His father had managed it but somehow it had eluded him no matter what he did. Could he ignore such antagonism though?

There was always someone wanting MacIntyre land for themselves. Either that or broaching his territory to steal livestock and grain. He had no idea how his father hadn't gone mad trying to keep on top of everything.

He looked at the men riding with him. He wished he could ask their counsel but he already knew what they would say. Gillis, his loyal deputy, by his side since childhood. He would tell him clan war was the only option. Derek would tell him the opposite, he would not want war with his own kin.

Derek was still technically a MacLeish. He'd been brought to MacIntyre castle by Duff MacLeish himself as a gesture of peace at the age of fifteen, marking the end of the last war.

Derek had changed a lot since then. A mere child when handed over, he'd sobbed and begged to be allowed to go home, promising his father he would behave.

"You'll stay here and do as you're told," Duff had replied, pushing him away, ignoring his tears. "You should have thought of repentance when you were gambling with my money. Perhaps you'll learn some courtly manners while you're at it. God knows, you never learned any from me. Twenty marks gone in a day and for what? Because you thought you had a decent dice roll coming up."

"Please, father. Don't make me stay here. I'm no MacIntyre. I'm a MacLeish like you."

"No MacLeish would act like you have. Look at you crying like a wee bairn. You shame me in front of another clan with your blather. You'll do this or you'll take monastic vows, I swear by God. I've had enough of your errant ways, my boy."

Andrew had watched the dynamic play out in front of him. He hoped if he ever had children they would get on better with him than the MacLeish boy did with his father.

Fifteen years had passed since then. He had no children, nor even the hint of a wife. Looking after the clan took up all his time. He had none spare to go courting. When younger he'd thought he would have all the time in the world to find a woman. He'd had to grow up fast when he inherited the lairdship upon his father's untimely death. Then all his free time vanished.

Derek had become a man too over the years though he still held stubbornly onto his refusal to wear the MacIntyre tartan. In the intervening years he'd become a surprisingly solid part of the clan, even if he was sometimes prone to acting higher than his position warranted.

"Do you need any help holding her?" Derek asked, nodding across at him. "She can sit on my lap if she wants."

The other men laughed but Andrew was in no mood for humor. "You think this is a time for jests? You keep your mouth shut and pray for those who are dying back there."

Derek turned away without another word, facing the front.

Andrew began thinking about what had just happened. He couldn't understand it. The MacLeishes had never done something so heinous before. Skirmishes maybe but there hadn't been war for fifteen years. Why provoke it after so long?

He glanced at the fair lass sitting in front of him on the horse. Maybe she'd be able to give him some answers.

Why would her people want to provoke a war they were sure to lose? There was no point asking Derek. He hadn't been back to MacLeish castle for years.

Did she not know provoking war was madness? MacLeish held lands half the acreage of the MacIntyres and their armed forces were outnumbered three to one. They would be slaughtered in a straight fight. He just couldn't fathom why they'd do it.

Could it possibly have been anyone else?

No, they'd all been wearing the MacLeish tartan. All apart from her.

What was she wearing anyway? He examined her attire more closely. She had on a skirt that exposed her knees like she was working the fields but with no hose underneath to hide her skin. And yet her shoes were intricate enough to look like she'd come from the very top of a Saracen court.

Her top was stranger still, a mixture of colors, blue and white with flowers sewn into the fabric and yet there was no sign of stitching of the emblems. Was she a jongleur perhaps? They often wore outlandish attire, brought back from their travels across Europe and the East.

He took a deep breath and as he did so, he caught the scent of her hair. Behind the lingering smell of smoke was something else, something much softer. What was that? He leaned toward her and sniffed. Lavender and heather in flower.

His horse tripped over a stone and almost stumbled. He admonished himself to concentrate on riding, not on what his captive smelled like. Why did he even care?

They made it to the castle by late afternoon. Once inside the courtyard he lifted the woman off the horse, setting her on her feet. "Hold there," he said to her before waving Gillis across. "Have her to change into attire more befitting a lady."

"I'll take her," Derek said. "I mean, you too have much to do to prepare for the wounded."

Gillis looked to Andrew. He nodded. "Very well. Gillis find Rory for me."

He watched the lass go, Derek shoving her hard whenever she slowed to look about her. He would have a word with him later, remind him that being rough with captives was not the MacIntyre way.

Turning, he saw his steward rushing over from the stables, doing his best to run. "I am glad to see you, Rory," Andrew said. "I will be brief as there is much to be done. The old hall has been burned as has half of Pluscarden."

"How bad is the damage?" That was Rory all over. Straight down to business every time, no room for sentimentality. That was why he made such a good steward.

"The hall is ruined as is half the village. I believe the rest would have gone up too if I was not there to scare them off."

"Who would do such a thing?"

"The MacLeishes."

"Are you certain?"

"Most of them escaped but we caught one of the villains. The wee lass should be able to prove it was them but we can discuss that later. For now, I need you to warn the infirmary and then the kitchens. We will have the entire village here by nightfall and many wounded among them. Have we enough food in the stores?"

"Aye, depending how long our guests will be staying."

"That I cannot answer."

"Should I send word to MacLeish that you would parley with him?"

"Not yet."

"A bath perhaps to remove all that soot from you?"

"Later. First I must speak to the apothecary. We will have need of many herbs before the day is out."

"Very good, my laird."

Rory scuttled off across the courtyard toward the infirmary. Andrew watched him go before heading for the keep.

She was up there waiting to be questioned. He thought of the scent of her hair and the feel of her skin as he'd lifted her from the horse. It had felt soft, softer than anything he'd ever known.

He dipped under the external staircase and into the cellarium. "James? Are you in there?"

"Aye. Back here. Hold on, I need to note the number of apples."

"Wounded are coming. I need you to prepare."

A bent figure appeared out of the gloom, wiping ink from his hands as he came into view. "How many?"

"At least a dozen, maybe more, all badly burned."

"God preserve us."

"I need you to help Him do that."

"I'll do what I can. How long do I have?"

"Not long. They're on their way from Pluscarden now."

"I will get all I can to the infirmary, my laird." He nodded and disappeared back into the darkness of the stores.

Andrew walked back outside. He was glad to have people he could rely on.

It was time to talk to his guest. He went to climb the stairs but heard his name being called behind him. "Derek?" he said, walking back down. "What are you doing down here? Have you left her alone?"

"I was looking for you. Dinnae worry, I've locked her in. She's going nowhere."

He frowned his disapproval. "She gave her word she would not run. You need not have imprisoned her. You were supposed to get one of the women to help her change attire."

"You are too trusting. It's by far your biggest flaw. She fears for her life, she'll run the first chance she gets, mark my words."

"Give me the key and stop making decisions for me."

Derek swallowed as if chewing something unpleasant. "Yes, my laird," he managed at last.

"The key, now. I wish to speak to her."

"So be it but be warned. She is a vicious one." He rubbed his cheek as he spoke and Andrew noticed a slight reddening to it.

He felt eyes on him from far above. Looking up he saw her at a window for a brief moment. Then it was gone.

"She will not be vicious with me," he said, taking the stairs two at a time. "I am sure of it."

Chapter Three

Beth stood in the chamber, her clothes on the bed. He was coming to see her. She didn't have long to get into the medieval dress. Anxiety gnawed at her. All she wanted was to find her mom and now she was locked in a castle tower and a brutish highlander was coming to interrogate her.

Derek had lied to her back at the old hall, telling her that her mother was waiting for her at the castle.

"She's up there in the solar waiting for you," he said as they crossed the courtyard. "Straight up the stairs."

She almost ran up the stairs to the second floor of the keep, turning sharp left at the end of a corridor and walking into a small room lit by a single window. There was no one waiting in there.

By the time she realized she'd been lied to, the door was locked behind her. "Hey," she shouted as it slammed shut. "You promised me she was here."

How could she have been stupid enough to believe it? No doubt he'd acted on the orders of the giant to keep her compliant and she'd been gullible enough to fall for it.

Her mind had been scrambled by the fire. That was the only possible explanation for falling for such a blatant lie.

She dashed over to the window and looked out. There would be no leaving that way. It was a sheer drop down to the courtyard far below. The shutter creaked in the wind as she looked out at the scene down there.

A part of her still believed it was all a re-enactment. She was surprised she'd not heard of it before. So much money had clearly been spent here making it all look authentic. It was like a movie set but with no camera crew to be seen.

Every single person down there was in period costume, all of them acting in the character of middle ages castle dweller. But where were the visitors?

Her mind went back to the journey, something niggling at her that she didn't want to think about. She'd sat in front of the actor who must have been playing the laird, him holding her firmly in place between arms of steel.

She looked at the surrounding countryside while they traveled. What was wrong with it? Something didn't add up. She couldn't work it out, finding it too hard to focus on anything but his chest pressing against her back.

It was the road, she realized whilst sitting in the tower. They'd come along a rough rutted track that was stone and mud, nothing else. There were no cars anywhere. No white lines or road signs.

Only the horses and the surrounding fields divided into long narrow strips. No walls, no hedgerows, just the fields and beyond them the imposing mountains.

Then the castle, looming up before them when they crested a hilltop. As it grew nearer she stared in disbelief. It looked so real, as if she had really gone back in time. The attention to detail was second to none. There wasn't a single cable or sign anywhere. Nothing modern at all.

The place itself clearly wasn't finished. Men were working on wooden scaffolding on the outer walls and piles of stone were dotted about on the ground. Lime pits smoldered and everywhere was the sound of hammering and chiseling. There were no drills though. They were using authentic tools to work on the walls.

The keep looked worse than the walls, the battlements and towers pointing upward like broken teeth high above her. The room she was locked in was complete at least but the plaster on the walls was bulging in places. If she'd been in charge, she'd have had words with the laborers about doing their job right. It hadn't been given enough time to set properly.

She looked around the room, hoping to find something that would help her escape. There wasn't much to see. A small bed frame of unvarnished wood, straw mattress on top. Blankets of itchy wool, dyed the same style of tartan that the re-enactors wore.

Next to the bed was a low table containing a candle, a large ewer of water beside it.

The only other furniture was a chair by the hearth and a faded woolen rug that covered less than a quarter of the flagstones.

She stopped her search when she heard a key turning in the lock behind her. She spun around in time to see Derek walking in, a pile of clothing in his arms. "I thought I'd bring the attire up here, save the women a climb up the stairs."

"Look, I'm not one of the re-enactors," she said. "You've got me mixed up. I'm a visitor, just a guest, that's all."

"Aye, you're a guest of the MacIntyres and you're to change into this."

"I will not change into anything. I need to find my mom. She'll be worried about me."

He shoved her backward, a warm smile spreading across his lips. "If you need some assistance in changing, I could always help you."

She knew then why he'd brought the clothes himself. He winked at her and reached out toward her chest. She batted his hand away. He lunged again and as he did so she slapped his face, hard. "Get your hands off me."

"You would strike a MacLeish?" he said in disbelief, rubbing his cheek. "You'll pay for that soon enough, lass."

"Enough. I'm not part of this game. You're holding me here against my will. That is a crime and if you don't let me out at once, I shall call the police and have you arrested."

"Call for whatever you like. No one will hear you from up here."

"I'm calling them right now," she said, reaching for her cellphone in her jacket pocket. She cursed as she realized it wasn't there.

Of course it wasn't. She's given her jacket to her mother to keep her warm in the cold Scottish air. No cellphone, no car keys, no way of getting help. Fantastic.

Derek was still looking at her. He lowered his voice. "I'm a MacLeish you know? I can help you if you let me."

"You can help me by getting out of my way. I'm not staying here a minute longer." She tried to push past him.

He shoved her backward and the door was shut before she had time to recover. She ran across and tried to get it open again but it was already locked. Hammering on the door, she screamed, "Let me out at once!"

There was no response, only retreating footsteps.

She crossed to the window and shouted, "Help!" No one even looked up. They were all clearly in on this together.

Was it not a re-enactment? She'd done a couple of escape the room challenges before. Was this the same kind of thing? Had her mother paid for it for her as some kind of surprise?

It was possible. The fire hadn't injured her. Could they fake a fire though? Of course they could, it happened all the time on TV. Were the victims just covered in special effects make up? Was that it?

She thought about what had happened so far that morning. They'd arrived at the old hall just after it opened, the first visitors to go inside. Her mother had been unusually excited. She'd thought it was just because she was seeing Andrew MacIntyre's birthplace but maybe it was because of this.

The smoke. Her mother had noticed it first. Almost as if she were expecting it. Then the flames and her moving through them to the outside, miraculously unhurt.

The men on horseback had appeared from nowhere which was very convenient as well.

Some had run into the fire without stopping. It was all starting to make some kind of sense. It was a set up. They'd brought out actors playing the wounded.

Had she actually seen anyone getting hurt?

No, not a single person. It all fitted her theory. This was just a game like that Michael Douglas movie or that other one, the Bill

Murray one set in London. The Man Who Knew Too Little. That was it.

It must have cost her mother a fortune for the tickets. All these people needed paying and all of them doing this just for her benefit.

She could have kicked herself for being frightened. None of this was real, it was just a game. She looked at the clothes Derek had left on the rug when he left. They looked so authentic. The attention to detail was incredible.

She thought about what she knew about medieval costume. Holding up each piece, she slotted them together in her head, trying to remember what her mother had said while they'd been going around the old hall.

No underwear but a long linen undergown. What was that called? A kirtle, that was it. Like a nightdress but almost reaching the floor. Then a dress of plain red wool, the hem of that would reach the floor. Several holes had been deliberately cut into the dress, she had no idea why.

Grey leggings called hose like the men wore. A wool belt known as a girdle back then. Black leather shoes like modern slippers but with the seams on the inside. Attached to the bottom of each shoe was a smooth wooden sole an inch high.

A white pillbox hat was in the pile too. Then a chin strap to hold the hat in place. That was a barbette, she remembered mom saying.

"Only married women had to cover their hair at that time," mom had said, pointing to the mannequins on display in the old hall. "But you were looked down on if you had your hair on display at all, especially in the noble families. They were quite lucky up in Scotland, lots of plants to dye the clothes. Down in England it was a lot more expensive to be so colorful."

Seeing outfits like that on a mannequin was very different to holding one in her hands. Was she supposed to put it all on and act like one of them? Could she at least get someone to break character and explain what she was supposed to do?

She looked out into the courtyard again. She saw Derek deep in conversation with Andrew, the laird, the man her mother had admired more than any other figure from the middle ages.

"He united an entire clan and then brought peace to the region for decades afterward," as she was so fond of telling Beth. "No other clan chief achieved as much for another hundred years."

Beth looked down at the actor playing him. From this distance she couldn't tell what he was talking about but she guessed it was her. Derek was gesticulating next to him, no doubt complaining about being slapped.

He seemed to make up his mind a moment later about something and marched toward the keep. Was he coming to her? He stopped again, turning back, continuing his conversation with Derek.

She had to decide quickly. Join in the game or tell him she wanted to cancel the whole thing. Mom had paid for it and would want her to enjoy it.

There was something else she needed to decide too. Should she change into the clothes they'd given her or remain in her existing ones?

Her mother had given her no clues about any of it, she never even mentioned an interactive game when they headed to Scotland together.

Two weeks looking at the sites her mother loved. That was all they were supposed to be doing. It might be their last chance. She was getting weaker all the time. It wouldn't be long before she lacked the strength for any journeys. It might be their last vacation together ever. That thought alone was enough to bring Beth close to tears.

She would join in, she decided at last. It would be what her mother wanted. She pulled her top over her head, tossing it onto the bed.

Crossing the room to the ewer, she sloshed water onto her arms, wiping away the worst of the soot. Returning to the bed, she undressed to her bra and panties before rolling the hose up her legs. They felt softer than she'd expected, more like leggings than pantyhose.

Once that was done she stepped into the kirtle. Over that went the dress, the kirtle visible in places through it. The dress fitted her surprisingly well, the hem brushing the floor until she put the shoes on, their wooden soles raising her in height at the cost of her ability to balance.

It took a while to get used to the feel of the shoes on her feet. When she finally felt able to stand without stumbling she turned to the hat, tying it to her head with the barbette in a neat bow under her chin.

She wished there was a mirror to see how she looked but maybe her mother could take a photo whenever they were finally reunited. She brushed the dress down, surprised by how comfortable the ensemble was.

She knew he was coming up. She could feel it in her bones. He was on his way up the stairs.

Still it came as a shock when she heard the door unlocking behind her. He was so tall he had to duck as he entered the room, only standing up straight once he was inside. He took one look and her and said, "Now you look like a proper highland lass."

Chapter Four

She looked like she'd lived in the castle forever. Andrew couldn't believe his eyes when he unlocked the tower to find her standing there like a true highland lass, fire in her eyes and standing like she was ready for a fight.

From what Derek had told him of her refusing to change, he expected an argument but nothing had prepared him for the sight of her in that dress that clung to her body so perfectly. He walked in to find her not only changed into the attire that had been provided but looking utterly ravishing.

Her hair was hidden under the filet but that meant her face had nothing to hide its beauty.

The dress fitted her as if it had been made just for her, the girdle gathering it in tightly at the waist. Through the carefully cut holes he could see hints of her kirtle. It was the latest fashion and he approved, at least on her.

It made him desperate to see more, exactly as the seamstress intended. Imagine seeing her in just the kirtle, he thought, then he imagined peeling even that layer from her, leaving her wearing not a single stitch of clothing.

He shook his head to clear his thoughts. It would never do to have such sinful desires for a MacLeish. People would talk. "I have sent word to your father."

"You'll be waiting a long time for a reply."

"Oh, and why's that? Think he'll disown your actions?"

"My father's dead."

"Duff MacLeish is dead?"

"No, Jonathan Dagless is dead."

He scratched his forehead. "Who's Jonathan Dagless?"

"My father. He died when I was ten."

"Are you saying your father is not Duff MacLeish?"

"That's what I just tried to tell you. Now just stop acting for a minute and talk to me about this game."

"This is no game lass."

"I know, I know. You're not supposed to break character. But I can if my mom's paying for this. I want to speak to her then I promise I'll be as medieval as you want. All bad teeth and swordplay. Whatever you need."

"I have no ken what you're blathering about but if you think I'm going to believe you're not a MacLeish when you were with those who wore their tartan, you're a fool."

"I'm not a MacLeish. I'm Beth Dagless. I'm twenty-three, I live in Surrey and I've been studying architecture for the last year with the Open University. I'm not a MacLeish, a MacDonald's burger or a

Cameron MacIntosh musical. I'm here with my mom and I'm worried about her. She's really sick, okay? So you can stop all this yay verily and hey nonny nonny and talk to me like a normal person or I'll be leaving a scorcher of a one star review on Tripadvisor about this castle and this game."

He sighed, examining her closely. "You use a lot of strange words, lassie, whoever you are. Tell me something."

"What?"

"If you're not a MacLeish, how do you explain coming out of my hall with one of their burning torches in your hand?"

"I was visiting with my mom."

"Does she work for me? I've not seen you before."

"No, listen. We'd come to see the birthplace of Andrew MacIntyre. Then I don't know, there was this fire all of a sudden. It was like a magic fire and then this tornado blew me outside and I'd grabbed mom's hand but it wasn't her hand, it was that torch you saw."

"Why did you come to see where I was born?"

"Sorry, what? That's what you choose to focus on? You are so self centred."

"Why did you come to see where I was born?"

"Look, I know you're acting. You're playing Andrew MacIntyre. I get it. You're the laird and all gruff but I'm not playing until I get to see my mom."

He stood tall, his voice loud enough to make her wince. "I am not acting anything. I am Andrew MacIntyre, laird of all these lands and the fair isles to the north of here."

"Right. Course you are. Look, I bet I can catch you out. What year is this?"

"The year of our Lord 1190."

"Okay then. If it's really 1190, who's the king?"

"William is once again king of Scotland though only after handing over a fortune to Henry last year like we still pay weregild to our tormentors, the deuced fool."

"You know your history. I'll give you that. Do they have some course you have to take before doing this?"

"Course?"

"You know, training you up so it's all believable. I know it's a game okay? There's no need to keep pretending."

"You still insist in this absurd nonsense of gameplay? I will prove this is real. Come with me."

He marched to the door, waving impatiently for her to follow. He didn't look back. He knew she would come after him.

*

Beth wasn't sure where he was taking her but anywhere was better than being locked in like Rapunzel. She followed him to the end of the corridor as he turned, and then headed downstairs.

As she descended, she noticed a smell so bad it almost knocked her over. "What is that?" she asked, trying not to gag as they walked along the corridor and out onto the balcony beyond.

"What? There was only the great hall back there? What of it?"

"You didn't notice that smell?"

He shook his head. "You are stalling. It will not work. Come see what kind of game you think this is."

He marched across the courtyard leaving her to follow. The hall had smelt so foul she gulped at the fresh air like a drowning sailor washed onto a beach after a storm. It smelled as if the hall had been used as a bin and toilet all at once.

The courtyard was little better. To her left clothes were draped over thick bushes of holly to dry but there was little chance of that in such damp air.

The mud was churned up from the passage of many feet and it was imbued with stink that clung to her nose and the back of her throat. Walking through the filth in her medieval shoes was not easy but she was more glad than ever for the wooden soles. They stopped the worst of it soaking into her feet and helped the hem of her dress remain relatively clean.

The actor playing Andrew opened the door to a building set against the castle wall, standing for a brief moment under the pentise overhanging the entrance. "In here," he said before vanishing.

It took Beth's eyes a moment to adjust to the gloom as she followed him inside. She heard crying and moaning up ahead of her in the darkness.

"Where are we?" she asked, blinking and through the gloom spying low beds laid out in a row along the wall. A figure occupied each one, some still, some writhing and moaning in agony.

"The infirmary," Andrew said, striding toward the nearest bed. "Does this look like a game to you?" he asked, pointing down at the woman laid before them, her face wrapped in clothes. What skin was visible was burning red and black.

An awful smell rose from the patient, far worse than that which came from the great hall.

Beth had to work hard not to gag as the woman shifted in place. Her mouth opened and a gout of blood spurted out like a fountain. "Rory," the actor shouted. "Mary needs your aid."

Out of the shadows a portly figure ran over, kneeling next to the bed, wiping blood from the stricken woman's lips. "Stay still," he whispered. "God is with you. Angels protect her."

The woman coughed again, her back arching as she did so. Then she fell back, a final wisp of air leaving her lungs. She was dead.

"Gone," Rory said, closing her eyes with his palm before getting to his feet. "May the Lord protect you and the angels watch over you."

"But...but this is just a game," Beth said, staggering backward toward the door. "She's just acting, right?"

Andrew looked furious. "I've known that woman all my life."

The whispering voice in the back of her head finally spoke loud enough for her to hear, though she still tried to ignore them. "This isn't a game," it said. "This is real and you better get used to the idea."

She'd always known of course, deep down. She'd just been trying her best to deny it. What was more likely? That this was an elaborate live action game involving a cast of literally hundreds, all set in countless acres of land? Or that she had somehow found herself in the actual middle ages?

Neither option seemed particularly plausible but the dead woman in front of her looked very real.

Had she died in the fire? Was this some elaborate version of heaven? No, if it was heaven, there wouldn't be mud on everything.

"This is real, isn't it?" she muttered, groping for the door, desperate for some air. "Oh, God. This is really happening."

She almost fell out into the open, grabbing hold of the wooden post that held up one corner of the pentise. A wave of dizziness washed over her. This wasn't a game. This was 1190 and that poor woman had just died from a fire they thought she'd help set.

This being the past meant two things. The man standing in the doorway looking out at her actually was Andrew MacIntyre, laird of the clan her mother loved so much. Perhaps she should ask him if he planned on marrying a Dagless. Maybe she'd meet her own great, great, great times however many great, grandmother here.

This being the actual middle ages meant something far worse than being stuck here. It meant she might never see her mom again. That thought brought tears to her eyes that she couldn't stop from falling as she gasped for breath, sinking to her knees, shaking her head in disbelief. "It can't be real, it must be a game."

"This is no game," Andrew said softly behind her. She looked up, expecting to see fury still plastered across his face.

Instead, he looked kinder, almost gentle. He held out a hand, lifting her slowly to her feet as she continued to pant for breath.

"The hall," she gasped, talking to herself as if he wasn't there. "It must be something to do with the hall and the fire. If I go back, maybe I can get back to her. She'll be worrying herself sick wondering where I am. I have to go."

She turned but he wouldn't let go of her hand.

"What are you doing? Let go of me? I'm going to look for my mom."

"It's not safe out there, lass. The MacLeishes are on their way and there may be a siege coming before long."

"So? What does that matter to me? Let me go."

He leaned toward her, lowering his voice. "There are others out there too. Those who might not be as kind as I've been."

"Kind? You lock me in the tower and won't let me leave your castle. How is that kind?"

"Kinder than letting my men toss you back into the blaze. Kinder than having you hanged for your part in murder. Kinder than letting you walk out while those from Pluscarden make their way here. Some of them may want revenge on those who burned down their village and I won't be able to stop them if I'm in here and you're out there."

"But I didn't do it."

He let go of her hand. "Aye. I think I believe you."

"All of a sudden, you just believe me?"

He shrugged. "You have honest eyes."

"So you'll let me go?"

He shook his head. "I said I believe you but I doubt they will. I'm doing this for your own safety." He waved at someone who was crossing the courtyard carrying a roll of parchment. "Finley, over here."

"I was just looking for you," Finley replied. "I have MacLeish's response to your missive."

"I will take it. Get Derek and get her into the tower."

"Aye, my laird. Derek!"

Beth turned and begged Andrew to let her go. "Please, don't do this. I need to go home."

"It's for your own good lass. You'll be safe here while we sort this affair out. I will not leave you long, I swear."

A look of sorrow crossed his eyes as he turned away, breaking the wax seal that held the letter shut and reading quickly.

Derek and Finley began dragging her away. She again called out to Andrew but he was walking away, ignoring her completely.

"Help me get her to the top of the tower," Derek said. "She'll not escape there."

"But that part's not finished. If she should escape..."

"If she plans to escape that way, it'll be by growing wings."

Beth tried once more to break free but more men appeared. She could only struggle as they dragged her kicking and screaming across the courtyard and into the keep. She fought them all the way up the stairs but it was no use. They went past the room she'd been in before and still they were going up.

At last they reached the top. She was pushed through a doorway into a half built room that was open to the elements, the wind blowing into it from two open sides. It was barely a room at all, lacking a roof and most of the walls. As Derek pulled the door closed, she hammered her fists upon it, demanding to be let out.

She was trapped once more and she no longer even had the comfort of thinking it was a game. It was real. She was really in 1190 and, like he'd said, unless she learned to fly, there was nothing she could do until someone came and let her out.

Once they did, she vowed never to let any of them near her again. She would run out of the castle gates and back to the hall. She held onto that idea like her mom would grip the locket when she was afraid.

If coming out of the hall had brought her back in time then it stood to reason that going back inside would return her to the present. She'd get back to her mom and have the chance to tell her just what Andrew MacIntyre was really like. He was a brute and she wanted nothing at all to do with him.

His smoldering eyes, his taut muscles, those broad shoulders that would make her feel so safe if he wrapped her in his arms. No, she didn't want anything to do with any of those things at all. Definitely not.

Chapter Five

Andrew rode out at the front of his men, the wind on their backs as they headed north. He'd brought half a dozen of his best out with him, leaving the rest to guard the castle. And her.

He could not be sure the MacLeishes wouldn't try to attack while he was on the way to their parley. If they did, he'd make sure he took MacLeish castle, truce or no truce.

Each of the warriors by his side was worth four of any other clan. That gave him good odds if they came upon anything up to two dozen on their journey. More than that? Any more than that and the heather would be nourished with MacIntyre blood and there was little he could do about it but die with honor like all MacIntyres when their time came.

From the castle they rode out through the rolling hills beyond, the road rising slowly to the first peak before he stopped. They looked back at the castle. It was covered in scaffolding. Would it ever be finished? The masons seemed to work slower and slower each day and unless he was there to watch them, little got done by the time night came.

Would the walls be done in time for winter? He hoped so. Needing to leave the mortar covered with great gaps during the long cold months was asking for trouble but what choice did he have? He needed a mason he could leave in charge while he was on the move, get them working faster. It was for their safety as well as his own. In a siege, none were safe.

He glanced up at the keep, faintly visible in the hazy distance. She was in there.

"Yon wee lassie will give you a kiss and a cuddle when we get back," Clyde shouted from the back of the group, as if reading his mind. "Dinnae think we can't see you staring back at her tower."

"Aye, he's got her locked in where she cannae escape his attempts at wooing," Wallace added.

"Dinnae joke about such things," Gillis spoke over their laughter. "Would any of you want to see your laird bed a MacLeish?"

"She's not a MacLeish," Andrew said, speaking for the first time since they left the castle.

"Och, who told you that?" Lorne asked. "Her by any chance?"

"Aye, she did."

"And you believe her? She's batted her eyelids at you and you go and fall for her charms without a moment's pause. Are you that desperate for a woman? There are plenty out there easier to conquer."

"I'd like to conquer her, I'll tell you that," Wallace shouted to more laughter. "Conquer her and her charms."

"Of course she's a MacLeish," Lorne continued, ignoring the interruption. "And I think we have a right to know what you're planning to do with her."

Andrew turned and gave him a firm look. "And since when do I have to explain myself to you?"

"You're asking us to ride out with you to meet Duff MacLeish. We might not live to ride back. Do you not think we should know what your plan is?"

A grumble of agreement.

Andrew sighed, too tired to argue. "We ride to the old hall. Duff MacLeish is meeting us there with no more than half a dozen of his men to parley. We'll see what he has to say about all this. He tells us why he felt the need to provoke war by burning the hall and then I decide what we do next. Anyone has any issue with that, I say we step off our horses and let our swords resolve the point."

Silence. No one mentioned Beth. Good, he didn't want to have to think about her. He needed to focus.

He pointed forward and they began to move again. Behind him the light was beginning to fade. They would be returning in the dark. A chill wind began blowing across the hill top. It would be a cold night. Would she be all right? Rory would hopefully arrange for her fire to be lit. Stop thinking about her, he told himself. He managed it eventually though he couldn't stop wishing he'd given her some furs to keep her warm while he was gone.

They descended slowly into the valley until the castle was out of sight behind them. Another hour or so and they would be at Ramshorn. Then a few miles after that they would reach Pluscarden, or what was left of it.

Ramshorn itself was on the edge of the wild moor. It was a single dwelling hidden from all those who passed by on the road. Only Andrew knew its exact location. He wanted it to always remain that way. He never intended to share it with anyone.

The sky had begun to turn shades of orange and red by the time they again stopped. "Hold here," he said, climbing down from his horse. "Keep a sharp eye out for an ambush. We are too close to the MacLeish border to relax. I shall not be long."

He left his men and headed off the road, walking at first through long grass and then into thicker undergrowth. Ahead of him was the tall slopes of a mountain, the top dusted with snow. It was a deceptive view for when he got closer, a hidden dip emerged at the base of the mountain. Trees shielded the dip from view and he had to push through the undergrowth between them in order to reach it.

There in the bottom of the valley was Ramshorn. Smoke was curling up through the thatch. That meant Fenella was home.

She was often abroad. There had been times he had gone to see her for advice only to find the house empty. When it mattered most though, she was always there as she had been since he was no more than a wee bairn. As long as he could remember he'd been brought to see her for advice.

He had no idea how old she was. For all he knew, she had been there forever, hidden from the clan feuds and boundary disputes, out of sight of the wars and battles, living out her quiet solitary life among the deer and the rabbits, advising one laird after another.

He was about to knock on her door when a voice called from inside, "Come on in, Andy."

He pushed open the door and waited for his eyes to adjust. She was sitting by the fire, two horn cups on the table in front of her. "Won't you join me for a drink?" she asked, sliding one toward him. "Fresh nettle tea."

He took the chair opposite hers, her cat immediately leaping onto his lap and curling up into a ball. He smiled, stroking its soft fur. "You know I don't let anyone else call me Andy."

"You want me to call you my laird? Bow and scrape to you? I didn't think you were one for such nonsense."

"You could at least pretend to have respect for my office."

"Och, I cleaned enough things from your tiny wee body when your father first brought you here to call you what I want. Or should I call you stinky drawers like your mother used to?"

He smiled. "It's good to see you."

"Is it? You do not look as if you're happy to be here. What brings the mighty clan chief out to the home of a dotty old witch anyway?"

"You're no witch." He took a sip of the tea. "Although I sometimes wonder how you always know when I'm coming."

"You're as noisy as a herd of cattle coming down that hillside. Now you didn't come here just to drink my tea and stroke old Podgorny. What's on your mind?"

Andrew drained his cup before answering. "Did you hear about what happened at the old hall?"

"Aye. Was a tragic business that and no mistake."

"I'm on my way to speak to Duff MacLeish about it."

"Oh. Why him?"

"Because it was his men who lit the fire."

"Was it indeed? Well, if you're so sure, off you go then and good luck to you."

"What do you mean?" He sat up straight in the chair. "Do you know something I don't?"

"All I know is the stars are aligning above us all and things are coming to a head for more than just you. Did you see the shooting star last night, flaming red as it fell?"

"No, was there one?"

"You should try looking up above your head sometime, Andy. It might do you some good."

She had a strange expression on her face. He was still trying to work out what she meant when she spoke again. "The omens are all there for those who know how to read them." She pointed to the ash that had fallen from the hearth. From his perspective it looked very much like it had formed the letter B. B for Beth.

"You know, don't you?" he said, leaning toward her. "You know about Beth. Who is she? Is she really from the future?"

"Time is not my concern, Andy. I only know that a wee lassie has taken hold of your heart and whoever she is, I hope she's worth the trouble that's come along with her."

"Trouble? What trouble?"

"I'm no oracle, Andy. I'm only a dotty old witch who needs her sleep. Your men will be waiting for you and I'm away to my bed. Off you go."

Podgorny jumped down from his lap and disappeared out the single window as if he'd been prodded with a stick. "Hunting mice," Fenella said by way of explanation. "Whatever happens, don't let the lassie go." She squeezed Andrew's hand so tightly he thought the bones would break.

How could one so small be so strong? "I thank you for your hospitality as always," he said, hovering on the threshold for a moment. "I never know what to make of the things you tell me."

"That's because I don't tell you anything you don't already know and you don't trust yourself as much as you should. Good night, my laird and remember, look up sometime."

"Good night, Fenella."

Dusk was approaching fast when he got back to his men. "What did she say?" Lorne asked, chewing on an oatcake as he spoke. "Are the omens good?"

"She thinks the blaze may not be the work of Duff MacLeish after all. She also thinks I should hold onto the lassie."

"If not MacLeish, who else would set the blaze?"

"I dinnae have a clue. Hush your talk for a wee spell. I need to think."

They rode on in silence. Another hour and they'd be at the remains of the old hall. What would he do if Duff MacLeish denied having any part in the fire?

He'd need to make a decision. Believe Duff and accept that he was no longer master of his own lands, open to attack whenever any stranger felt like it. Or start a clan war he didn't want. Neither option felt great. Trust your own feelings," she'd said. He glanced up at the darkening sky over his head. And look up sometime.

It was times like this he wished his father were still around. The burden of being laird weighed heaviest in these most difficult moments. Make the wrong choice and many of his people would suffer needlessly.

They rode in silence, the only sound that of hooves upon the damp ground. Behind them the sun dipped slowly out of sight below the horizon. In the last of the light Andrew caught sight of the remains of the old hall in front of them.

Duff MacLeish was already there, waiting with six of his men, all on horseback, none smiling. Andrew rode steadily toward him. It was time to get some answers.

Chapter Six

Beth watched them go from the top of the half built tower. She hated herself for even thinking about him. He'd ignored her perfectly reasonable request to get back to her own time and her mother who was no doubt waiting for her. Why couldn't she stop thinking about his hand slipping into hers outside the infirmary?

She didn't belong in the past. It was different when she'd thought it was maybe a re-enactment or a live action game. The reality meant being away from home, from finishing her course, from maybe one day becoming an architect like she'd always dreamed.

Far below her, he was riding out with six of his men. People moved out of the way so he could ride through the gate and then beyond the walls. Her eyes moved onto the surrounding countryside.

The riders headed slowly up a slope, pausing for a spell at the top to look back. They were no more than dots from this distance but she could have sworn he was looking right at her in that moment. Then they vanished over the crest and she felt more alone than she had in her entire life.

She hated herself for thinking about him after he'd gone. He didn't deserve her thoughts. He was rough, ignorant, rude, and...and impossibly handsome.

She sighed, moving away from the jagged edge of the tower wall into the safer space near the door.

It looked as if work had been stopped for some time. The floor was made of rough boards with inch thick gaps between them, revealing the floor below. She tried to lift them but they were nailed solidly in place. The walls were unplastered.

On two sides the stonework was complete, presumably where they connected to the interior space of the keep. The remaining two sides faced out into the open.

There were the remains of stumps that held the scaffolding in place but the thought of using them to climb down was enough to make her feel queasy. It was too high up and what if she fell? Her mother would never know what happened to her. She would just be one of the countless people who went missing each year, never to be heard from again.

The roof had yet to be built. The gap allowed the chill evening wind to blow through without anything there to prevent it. Had he told them to lock her in this awful prison?

She wanted to stop thinking about him. She wanted to think about getting home. She wanted to be at home in her armchair, her mother there but without the diagnosis looming over her. The two of them would sit together in silence, both reading. Mom would read about genealogy or Scotland and she'd have her architecture books.

That was a safe place. No blood spurting from dying people, no blazing infernos, and definitely no brutish giants in baldrics and hose locking her away to freeze to death.

She curled up in the corner by the door, wrapping her arms around her, trying and failing to keep warm.

With her eyes shut, his face came unbidden into her mind. What was it about him? She realized that despite everything that had happened to her, she'd felt safe around him. Until she was trapped in an unfinished tower at the top of the keep.

She opened her eyes to shake away the image of him wrapping her in his arms, an image she wanted to ignore. Her keen eyes ran over the jagged unfinished walls in front of her. Unable to stop herself, she started seeing it from an architectural point of view and what she saw scared her. It wasn't strong enough. The mortar had not set properly and was already crumbling. That meant the top layers of stones were weighing too heavily on the lower courses.

A closer look and she was proved right. The mortar had been pressed out by her feet, stone touching stone. That gave it no flexibility. If the winds were strong enough that section of wall would give way almost at once. If the rest of the keep had been built the same way then Andrew might not need a siege to bring down his castle. The winter weather might be enough to send it crashing down to the courtyard below.

She jumped up when a key rattled in the lock. The door opened a moment later and Derek walked in, a smirk on his face. "How are you enjoying your accommodation?"

"If that's a joke, I don't find it very funny. Have you come to let me out?"

"I'm to keep a close eye on you while you're here. I wondered if perhaps you might prefer to join me in my own chamber?"

"You have a room of your own?"

Beth didn't know a huge amount about medieval history but she knew that only the lord's family had private rooms in castles in this era. Everyone else slept together, usually in the great hall. The thought of the hall was enough to make her nose wrinkle in disgust.

"I am the son of a laird. Do you not think I warrant a chamber of my own? Lovely warm fire in there. Do you want to join me or not?"

"I'd rather stay here."

"Suit yourself," he snapped, pulling the door closed once more.

Beth sank once more to the ground, curling up and shivering uncontrollably. She thought about the fire she'd been offered and could almost feel the warmth sinking into her frozen bones. Then she thought of Derek, the curl of his lips when he looked at her, the way he kept glancing at her chest, how his hands had tried to touch her before. She knew she'd made the right decision.

An hour or so after sunset, the steward she'd seen talking to Andrew appeared in the doorway holding a tray of food. "I was told you were up here," he said, passing her the tray. "But I did not believe it. I am most sorry you are being treated this way, lass."

She grabbed a hunk of bread from the tray, surprised by how hungry she suddenly felt. "Thank you," she said, shoving a piece into her mouth. It tasted gritty. She found it hard to grip the rest in her frozen hands and her teeth chattered as she ate, making it hard to swallow.

"My name's Rory by the way," he said as she ate. "If you're a MacLeish I shall eat my baldric."

"How do you know I'm not a MacLeish?" she asked, looking at the warm face above her.

"I might be old but my eyes and ears still work well enough. You thanked me for the bread. You had a smile for me when you first saw me enter here. You're a gentle lass. If I didn't know better, I'd say you came from the royal court. There's grace in your soul. And fire too."

"I wish there was fire," she replied, picking up something purple. "What's this?" she asked, turning it over in her hand.

"Carrot," he replied. "Have you not seen one before?"

"Yes but...never mind. Can I ask you a question?"

"Aye."

"Why is the castle in such poor shape?"

"What? In what way?"

She chewed on the carrot for a moment, surprised by how sweet it tasted. Once she got over the difference in color, she could almost imagine she was eating it as part of a warm meal at home. The thought was comforting.

"There were wooden props holding up your portcullis. One small fire and the whole thing could be pushed over by two men. The battlement walls are too thin, I can tell that from here. They could easily be undermined.

Same with the keep. If the rest has been so thinly done as this room, the whole thing might collapse. Feel that mortar. It's too poor a quality for a wall such as this, nor has it been lain thick enough for such heights. In other places it is too thick. Your masons have been far too slapdash. And what building is that down there?"

He looked where she was pointing, a shocked look on his face. "The chapel, why?"

"The roof isn't aligned right. God help you if you get a strong winter wind.

"How do you know all this?"

"I learned it."

"Where?"

"Where I came from," she replied after a moment, not sure how much to share. "Will you tell your laird?"

She thought about the castle coming under siege as he had warned. When she first arrived she hadn't given much thought to the flaws, assuming they were because it was a recreation, not the real thing. Knowing this castle was built for defense made things different. She couldn't live with herself if she went home knowing there were easily fixable problems and she'd chosen to ignore them to save her own skin.

Rory looked out of the gap in the wall, crumbling a little of the mortar in between his fingers. "What would you do to fix these problems if you were master mason here?"

"You might not like hearing this."

"Go on."

"Well, first I'd sack your master mason."

Rory suppressed a smile. "Go on."

"Then I'd deal with defense first as winter's coming. I'd get the wooden props either buried or hidden behind strong stone walls. Long term you'd want to rebuild the keep and the walls of the battlements but for now you could thicken them at the bottom and at least get a single skin along the top after pulling the top couple of courses down. It would give the impression of level and concurrent strength to anyone outside. Might be enough to put them off if they don't get too close. Then come the spring, I'd pull it all down in sections and rebuild thicker and this time do it right."

"Would that not cost a fortune in stone?"

"Not really. You'd be able to reuse a lot of what you have as it's already dressed. You'd just need more rubble for infill and if that's hard to find you could deepen the earthworks and use what you dig out from there. You're on top of stone here, aren't you?"

"Aye. So we simply rebuild the entire keep and the walls. What about the chapel? Why do we need to fear the wind?"

"The roof is only half done but there's no point finishing it as it is. Leave it off center like that and it'll collapse in the first strong gale. The strength of a building like that comes from its symmetry. Same as the biggest cathedral.

It needs buttresses and the roof redoing entirely. Get that wood off and get someone who knows what they're doing to do it right. Whoever you hired for the work is taking you for a ride."

Again, a suppressed smile. "What about you?"

"What do you mean, what about me?"

"Could you do it?"

"Probably but I'm not-"

He interrupted her. "Me and you are going for a tour around the castle. You're going to point out every flaw you can find and in return I'll find you more salubrious accommodation. How does that sound to you?"

Beth nodded, unable to resist a smile.

"Why do you look so happy all of a sudden?" he asked, holding the door open for her to walk into the corridor beyond.

"I've always wanted to design a castle," she said over her shoulder, thinking of the cardboard and sticky tape constructions of her childhood.

He smiled back. "Now you might get to do it for real. But you'll have to fire the master mason first and that's going to be an interesting conversation."

Chapter Seven

It stabbed Andrew in the heart to see the hall of his childhood in ashes, scorched into the earth as if it had never been. The only thing left standing was a single doorway that once led into his bedroom. It looked like a perverse monolith, like it had been spared by God when all around had been burned.

He had seen many buildings burnt and replaced in his lifetime but never one that meant so much to him. The corridors he had run down as a bairn, pretending he was laird of a kingdom full of dragons and princesses.

Or the later times, seeing his father planning the castle, that cough wracking him as he leaned over the parchment, calculating figures in his head, trying to work out how he was going to pay for all the work that needed doing. All that was left was in his memory. All because someone wanted to start a war.

Was it Duff MacLeish? He looked at him, a space of open ground between them. Following the age old ritual, he held his sword aloft for a moment and then tossed it onto the ground. Duff did the same and only then did the two lairds dismount.

Duff had fifteen years on Andrew, his beard turning gray, his hair thinning. He still carried himself as tall as ever. Or did he? Was there just a hint of a slight stoop as he walked into the middle of the clearing.

"You called me out to parley," MacLeish said, his voice cold. "You bring me out from the warmth on a chill enough night to freeze a cat's arse. You better have good reason."

"Aye, that I have," Andrew replied. "Let us break bread together."

The ritual completed, they each collected their swords and waved to their men. Soon a circle of seated figures was in place on the grass. Andrew remembered watching many meetings take place this way.

He had asked his father why they were not held inside. "Would you want to sit in the hall of an enemy with no easy escape route?" was his answer. "The outdoors suit all highlanders for such purposes. It has always been this way."

Andrew sat opposite Duff, meeting his eye, not looking away, wanting to see how he reacted when the accusation was made. "You see the remains of my father's hall behind you."

"Aye." MacLeish's face gave nothing away. Next to him, his men watched closely, their hands too near their swords for Andrew to let down his guard.

"The men who burned the hall and the village wore your tartan."

"Did they now?" MacLeish said, sounding surprised. "And I suppose you think if I were responsible, I'd be foolish enough to send them out wearing it?"

"Are you saying you dinnae have any part in this?"

"Come on, Andrew. I like a straight fight like any man. I'm not a MacKenzie. I'm no coward who burns the homes of serfs to make a point. I'd rather take a castle with honor same as you."

Andrew saw the subtext clear as day. "Is that a threat?"

"Your temper'll be the death of you, laddie. I'm not the one accusing another of burning a village. You impugned my honor first, you dragged me out from my fireside because you had something vital to discuss according to your letter.

I come and I find I'm here to be accused of this? And then you accuse me of threatening you? If you want peace, this isnae the way to go about getting it."

"You swear on the Lord that you had nothing to do with the blaze?"

"Aye though that's not the question you should be asking."

"What is the right question?"

"You might ask me who else might want to provoke a clan war between the MacLeishes and the MacIntyres. Who stands to gain most if we're battling each other."

It came to Andrew in a flash. "The English."

"Aye, laddie. The Normans have been testing the border all along my land for months. What's to stop them putting on my tartan to get us nice and distracted by our own feuds? Did you catch any of them?"

He thought of Beth before shaking his head. "No, not one."

"Really? I heard you'd caught a lassie with a torch in her hand."

He shook his head again. "Don't believe everything you hear, Duff."

"It could be the MacKenzies of course. They've sent plenty enough of their bairns to the Norman court this last year. I wouldnae put it past them to be working with the English."

"But why? No highlander would ever..."

Duff managed a cold laugh. "The innocence of youth. So trusting. If we're at war, they join up with the Normans and sweep the north clean, take my land and yours for themselves and divide it up with the English."

Duff took a bite of the bread he'd been given. Andrew did the same. The meeting was over.

All the men were on their feet a second later, backing slowly from the clearing, watching each other intently.

Andrew did not turn his back until he was sure the MacLeishes were gone. Only then did he relax, breathing out heavily as his men muttered amongst themselves.

"What now?" Gillis asked as Andrew mounted his horse.

"We go home. I dinnae trust him not to ambush us in the dark. We ride fast. Keep a keen ear out for MacLeish archers."

"And what of the words he spoke?"

"I dinnae ken. You think he spoke the truth?"

"I only ken he has more to lose from clan war than us."

The men mounted up while Andrew turned his horse toward the castle. He rode as swiftly as he dared in the dark. Though he knew the route well, he dared not risk his horse falling in one of the many potholes and ruts that littered the road. Making the surface of better quality was just one more thing on his list for the future.

He needed to decide what he was going to do next. It did look as if Duff MacLeish was telling the truth. If that was the case then bigger problems were just around the corner. The castle was in no fit state to defend itself against the might of the Norman forces.

He remained lost in thought for most of the return journey, only brought out of his reverie when he spotted bright lights ahead of him. "Are there torches on the walls?" he asked, squinting and trying to make sense of what he was seeing.

"Aye, looks like it," Gillis replied.

"Did you order them lit?"

"Nay, my laird. I said nothing before we went. Rory perhaps?"

Andrew kicked the sides of his horse, sending it ahead of the group until he could make out what was happening. He came to a halt about fifty yards from the gate. The place was a hive of activity and none of it made any sense. People were milling around the portcullis, a pile of stone beside them. To the left, part of the wall had been torn down and more was being tossed down from one laborer to the next, stone by stone. Had there been a battle? If so where were the dead? Why was the portcullis still open?

In the earthworks people were digging out stones and handing them up the steep sides to others stood by carts. What was going on?

He rode up to the portcullis and had to slow to make his way through, the crowd too thick to notice him until he was on top of them. "Make way for your laird," Gillis called from behind him.

He was already through them before they even knew what was happening. Was he no longer in charge of his own people?

Calling out for a stableboy, he jumped down to the ground and caught sight of Rory in the distance, the torch in his hand lighting his face in the darkness. "Rory," he called, waving him over.

"My laird," Rory replied, scurrying across. "I expect you have some questions."

"Perhaps you might explain why my walls are two feet lower than I left them."

"About that-"

"Then you can explain why men are digging in the earthworks."

"Well, you see-"

"And then after that you can tell me why the portcullis is wide open and lit up like the noon day sun. Are we no longer taking precautions at night?"

Rory began to talk but Andrew wasn't listening. He was staring in disbelief at a tent that had been set up at the base of the walls. Out of it a woman had just walked and she was lit by the orange and yellow glow of the torches, making it look as if her hair was on fire.

It was her.

He silenced Rory with a wave of his hand. "Why is my captive over there with a line of men listening to every word she says?"

Rory at least had the decency to look sheepish, not meeting Andrew's eye. "You might want to come and meet your new master mason."

Andrew almost laughed. Then he saw the look in Rory's eyes. "You are jesting, are you not?"

"Nay, my laird. She may be a woman but she knows more about building methods than any man I have ever met. Every question I asked, she could answer. I tested her well but she knows far more than me. Some of her ideas are...well, they're quite

71

revolutionary. She said the walls were on the verge of collapse and I had no reason to doubt her. I thought you would want us to set to work fixing them at once especially if your talk with MacLeish fared ill."

"She said they were on the verge of collapse?"

"Aye."

"And you believed her just like that? A woman with no apprenticeship behind her and no tools of the trade brought with her?"

"Aye, my laird."

"Rory. I am going to wash and you are going to send her to me for a wee chat about this. And go find Derek while you're at it, I need a word with him too."

He walked across the courtyard. More scaffolding had been set up against the wall of the keep. Of course. Why not? Even the chapel had sounds of wood sawing coming from it. He thought about ordering all to cease but knew at once it would make him look weak, as if he were not in charge of his own people.

She would have some explaining to do when she came in. First, he needed to wipe the dirt of the trail from his face. He walked up the stairs and into the keep, passing into the great hall, the rushes rustling as he kicked through them. Few were asleep in there. It seemed as if most of the castle were working. How was he expected to pay for their labor?

He felt suddenly very tired and the last climb up the few steps to his solar above the great hall was hard work.

Once there he poured water from the ewer into the bowl beside it. All he could hear was the sound of hammering and talking outside.

Pulling his baldric from his body, he folded it and laid it on the bed. Kicking off his shoes, he stood on the rug and leaned on the table for a moment, gripping it in his fists.

How dare she tell them to pull down his walls and how dare they just do it as if he didn't matter anymore.

He felt furious with her in that moment. Splashing water onto his face, he rubbed his skin, scraping away the dirt from his chest with a strigil.

He heard a knock behind him and turned to find her standing in the doorway. The fury left him in an instant, replaced by a warmth that spread from his heart to his very fingertips, sweeping away the tiredness and making him feel very awake indeed.

"You sent for me," she said. "I expect you have a few questions."

"Aye lass," he said, beckoning her inside. "More than a few."

Chapter Eight

Beth knew she would need to explain herself. When Rory called for her to go across to the solar above the great hall, she knew why at once. "Is he angry?" she asked, unable to read the steward's expression.

"If he yells at you, send for me. I'll soon talk some sense into him. Without you, we might be looking at many dead and crushed when the place collapsed and I thank the Lord you came when you did to prevent such a disaster."

"I'll be over in a minute," she said, looking the endless queue of people, all with questions for her about the work. "I just need to set a few more things on the go."

"You better be quick. Keeping a laird waiting is not advisable."

She hurriedly called the queue together and then spoke to them all at once. "I shall be back as soon as I can. Hold for a short time."

She left them by the tent and crossed the courtyard to her reckoning.

She had got the hang of the wooden soles of her shoes in the time she'd been supervising the rebuild. That was something at least.

The noise of work carried on behind her. It surprised her how pleasing a sound she found it. She hadn't been expecting things to happen so quickly. It had been made abundantly clear when she began studying architecture that nothing in the building world happened fast. Here, she had shown the steward what needed doing and almost at once the demolition had begun.

Up the stairs, she paused, looking back at the work. The scaffolding next to her ran up to the unfinished towers. They needed pulling back and part of the wall taking down but no one was willing to get started on that yet without the laird's say so.

The walls had been an easier sell although less at risk of collapse. People were working hard. Progress would be swift. She just hoped it would be worth it and that Andrew could be made to see the value of what they were doing beyond the cost in pence.

She headed inside, making her way into the great hall. Pulling back the curtain she stepped through, the smell not seeming as strong as before. Was she just getting used to it?

Everything here was more intense, the smells, the sights, the sounds, all so much stronger than she was used to.

Everyone seemed to know each other too which was hard to accept at first but then the population of the country was what? A couple of million? Certainly fewer than in a single city in her time.

At the far end of the great hall was an open door. She passed through that and up a short flight of stairs. Turning a corner she walked straight into the solar before she even knew she'd reached it.

She stopped dead at the sight before her. Andrew was running wet hands through his hair, his eyes closed. From where she was he seemed to be nothing but shoulders and chest. His hose was sitting just above his hips, giving her a hint of what lay hidden inside, the water soaking through the fabric made it cling to every part of him. She couldn't move, she couldn't speak, she couldn't look away. All she could do was stare at the bulge.

"Beth," he growled, wiping his eyes with a cloth. "Come in and sit down lassie. We need to talk."

"Do we?" she replied.

"Please," he added, pointing to the chair by the fireside. He took a cloth and wiped his face.

Forcing her feet to move, Beth made it over to the chair, willing her eyes to only look at his face, nowhere else.

He crossed in front of her to poke at the fire, bringing it back to life. From where she was sitting his bulge was right in front of her face.

She closed her eyes and kept them shut until he moved away, her body heating up uncontrollably. She told herself it was the fire that was causing it but as he looked at her, the churning feeling deep inside her spoke the truth.

"I hear you've been making a few changes to my castle?"

"Stopping it from falling down. Your masons have done poor work." That wasn't how this was supposed to be begin. What was to gain from criticizing him?

"Want to tell me why I shouldn't have you chained up for bewitching my people into tearing down their own walls?"

"Feel free but I think they might have something to say to you about it."

"Like what?"

"Like that I'm strengthening your walls so they don't collapse. Or they might mention that the portcullis will stand up to a siege where it wouldn't before. Or maybe they'll tell you that you need a master mason who knows his stuff. No one will tell me who's been in charge of the building work so far. Will you? Whoever it is, their incompetence has left lasting damage and I want a word with them."

"Aye, maybe I'll tell you who's in charge."

"So who was the idiot you hired?"

"Me."

She felt a sudden lurch in her stomach. "You? You've been in charge of the building work? But you're the laird?"

"Aye. Are you saying I've not been doing a bonny job?"

"You've been doing an appalling job. On your watch the laborers haven't bothered mixing the lime mortar right. Your battlements have crumbled and you'll be lucky if they survived the winter. The roof of your chapel is about to collapse and as for your keep? If I were you I'd be pulling the whole thing down and starting again."

"My father designed this keep," he said, his voice quieter than before. "I only want to finish what he began."

"Then you need someone to supervise the building work. That's what a master mason does."

"I know what a master mason does. How do you?"

"Rory was telling me all about it."

"So tell me."

She told him everything she'd told Rory. She told him how they could use the stone dug out of the earthworks as rubble infill. She told him if he got this right, the laborers he was paying to do little could get the work done in months and get started earlier on Pluscarden abbey which she'd read in the guidebook he wouldn't found until 1195.

She told him how with the makeshift repairs his battlements would still dominate the landscape until spring when they could be rebuilt properly. She told him how to create a camber on the roads leading up to the castle to help with drainage. She told him how his enemies could easily undermine the place in any siege unless he got everything fixed quickly. There had not been the time to wait for his approval. It had to start at once.

Through it all he sat and listened quietly, not saying a word.

She only stopped talking when she realized someone was standing in the doorway. She looked up at the same time Andrew did to see Derek moving from the shadows into the room.

"How long have you been skulking?" Andrew asked.

"Not long," he replied. "I didnae want to interrupt the lassie. Sounds like there's some work to be done."

"What do you want, Derek?"

"You sent for me."

"What? Oh, aye, I did. Gather the men in the great hall. I need to talk to them."

"All the men?"

"Actually, on second thoughts leave those who are working for Beth."

"Working for her?" Derek's eyebrows raised momentarily before lowering again.

"Aye. Now on you go. I'll be down presently." He waited a moment before turning his attention back to Beth. "I hate how he walks around without making a sound. It's unnerving. Now, lassie, I wonder whether you'd consider being master mason of the castle until this work is done? I'd want you to rebuild my old hall too, if we can spare the wood for it."

Beth couldn't help it. She burst into tears. She tried to stop them but she was unable to do anything but let it happen.

Andrew was across the room in a moment, his arm on her shoulder. "What's the matter, wee lassie? What ails you?"

"It's nothing," she replied, feeling the heat of his hand through her dress, wanting it to go and stay in equal measure.

She couldn't tell him the truth. What good would it do? How could she tell him about her love of masonry and architecture? How it was the only thing she'd ever wanted to do? How her father had tried to tell her it was a man's job and she needed to set her sights on something more realistic? How she had to take a job to support her mother instead of going to college at the same time as everyone else from her school? How she'd finally started studying and still worried no one would give her a job? How many people out there thought it was just a man's job?

Yet here, in the era most people would consider far more sexist than her own, she was being offered the highest possible position a laird could offer apart from steward. She would be in charge of the entire rebuilding of the castle, maybe the old hall too. "Was the old hall all wood?" she asked, wondering about something as she sniffed loudly.

"Aye. Why'd you ask?"

"In my time it was stone vaulted."

"Never been vaulted in stone. Perhaps it could be if you took on the job?"

She almost cried again but managed to stop herself. She noticed his hand was still on her shoulder and he was leaning closer to her. She looked deep into those eyes which reflected the fire beside her. "I thought you'd be angry with me for starting work already. Then you act like this. I don't understand you at all."

"Maybe you could get to understand me better." He was leaning closer still. Another inch and his lips would touch hers. She yearned for him to do it, from deep inside all she wanted was to feel his lips on hers. He was going to do it. He was moving closer. She held her breath, leaning forward in her chair.

"The men are ready, my laird," a voice said loudly from the doorway.

At once the expression on Andrew's face changed. He stood up and was once again the brutish angry giant she'd first seen. "Good," he said, nodding to Derek who was looking from her to the laird and back again.

He left without saying another word, leaving Beth to sit in the solar and stare at his bed. She looked at it without moving for a very long time, lost in thought.

Chapter Nine

Beth looked out from the top of the scaffolding at the wall beyond, waiting for the wind to die down. It had been the first time she'd climbed so high and she was already regretting it. All that was keeping her from plummeting thirty feet to the ground was twine and rough wood planks that swayed alarmingly in the breeze.

Rory had promised her it was perfectly safe, inviting her to join him at the top to look over the work that had been done so far.

"What do you think?" she asked, turning to face him. "Does it meet your approval?"

"Aye," he replied, running his hand along the stone. "The laird will be pleased."

"Where is he anyway? I haven't seen him for a fortnight." As she said it, Beth felt a pang of guilt. That was more than two weeks since she'd seen her mother. It was almost as long since she'd thought about her. She'd been so caught up in all the building work that she'd had no spare time to think about anything else. Autumn was rapidly heading toward winter. Another week or two of work was the most they could do. Then the mortar would need to be covered up or the frost would damage it before it could set properly. Allow that to happen and the place would be crumbling all too soon and she couldn't see that happen.

She had come to the conclusion that maybe she'd been brought back in time to oversee this project. It would be a heck of a thing to put on her resume when it came to applying for jobs in the future.

"Have you got any experience of building work?"

"Oh yes, I helped redesign and fortify a Scottish castle."

"Great, and when was that?"

"Eight hundred years ago."

She smiled at the thought but her smile faded when a gust of wind made the scaffolding under her creak alarmingly.

She turned to look at Rory who seemed completely undisturbed. "Would you mind if we continued this conversation down in the courtyard?"

"Of course. After you."

She descended slowly, clambering down the layers of scaffolding, praying as she did every time that she wouldn't slip and lose grip. By the time she was standing on firm ground her arms ached from the effort of gripping so tightly. Rory caught up with her a minute later, craning his neck for a last look upward. "You're the master mason we've needed," he said, confirming her theory.

She was back to get the castle sorted and then she could go home. She had tried to overcome the guilt about her mother by rationalizing about time travel. If she went back through the doorway that had brought her back, logic dictated she would return to the exact moment she left. A bit like Return to Oz or The Lion, The Witch, and The Wardrobe, she'd be back in the present at the same time she left and no one would even know she'd been gone.

"They're trying the vaulting you suggested," Rory said, bringing her attention back to him. "At the old hall, I mean."

She smiled. It gave her a headache to think about it too much. In the present day the old hall had stone vaulting and she had been impressed by it. Then she found out the hall had burned because it was made of wood and her advice to vault it in stone was being followed. It would fireproof the building and strengthen it so it would last for centuries, long enough for her to marvel at her own work in the future without even realizing she was responsible.

"It would be a lot simpler to supervise if I was allowed to go there myself," she replied. "Make sure it's going the way it should."

"They are following your instructions. Springers, voussoirs, keystone. Falsework to hold it in place. There is no need for you to attend."

"Still, it would be nice." She looked at him and his eyes darted away. "Why does he insist on me staying here?"

Rory managed to glance at her before looking away again. "We should check on the falsework in the chapel."

84

She didn't press the subject. She had told Andrew the truth. She needed to go through the doorway in the old hall to get back to her own time. He had not responded but the same day the order went out that she was not to leave the grounds of the castle. He'd said it was to keep her safe while they tried to establish who had ordered the burning of Pluscarden but she suspected there was more to it than that. He didn't want her to go. She wanted it to be because of the kiss they'd so nearly shared but he'd been gone ever since then so she'd had no chance to talk about it with him. In the time he'd been gone she became less and less sure about how he felt. Was he just keeping her there for her skills as master mason? Was she imagining that he had feelings for her?

"Come on then," she said, heading across the courtyard. "Let's go take a look."

As they walked she glanced over at the portcullis. It was opening. Someone on horseback rode through a second later. She couldn't help smiling at the sight. He was back.

*

Andrew took one look at her standing in the middle of the courtyard and his heart soared. He had missed her terribly while he'd been away. Patrolling along the border with his men, he'd been looking for any signs of Norman forces. He'd found a few campfires but nothing more.

On the way back he'd stopped at Pluscarden to check on the progress. The ruins from the fire had been cleared away and the masons and laborers had worked fast. Dressed stone from the dismantled battlement walls of the castle had been brought by cart and were already forming the outline the building would take. The vault that would cover the cellarium had begun and he marveled at the speed of the work. "The difference a master mason can make," Gillis said, bringing his horse alongside.

"I can hardly believe it."

"Where is she? Is she not supervising?"

"I left her at the castle. She is safer there if the miscreants should return."

That was true but it wasn't the whole truth. He thought about her continual assertion that she had traveled through time to help him. There were elements of her that didn't add up. The clothing she had worn when they first met, the fact she knew so much about modern masonry techniques, even suggesting dog tooth stone carvings for extra strength in window and door lintels. It was her idea to cover the cart wheels with metal so they lasted longer. Was that enough to believe she was from eight hundred years in the future? Of course not.

He had come to two conclusions. One, she had traveled abroad. Rory had mentioned the term dog tooth when talking about some of his brothers who had traveled on the last crusade. She had clearly picked up her ideas from her travels. Two, she was quite mad. That was the only realistic explanation for her belief that passing through the one remaining doorway from the old hall would send her back to the future.

That was the main reason he had insisted she remain at the castle. To bring her to the hall would likely increase her madness. Would her mind snap entirely when she walked through it and nothing happened? He could not bear the thought. Better she remained safe in the castle, safe from men with burning torches and safe from the demons that lurked in her mind, trying to take over her soul.

"Should we get home?" Gillis asked, his horse flicking its mane under him.

"Aye," he said, turning from the hall and leading his men onto the track that led back to the castle. "What do you think of her?" he asked Gillis as they made their way steadily south. They had fallen behind the other highlanders who were talking amongst themselves.

"Beth?" Gillis asked.

"Aye."

"I think if she told you the truth, then God sent her to you for a reason."

Andrew nodded in response. "I want you to keep what I said between us."

"You still think she's mad?"

"I dinnae ken."

"What about her prophecy?"

"About Melrose Abbey? I have heard nothing."

"You could ask MacLeish if he's founded an abbey. That would not give too much away."

"And if he becomes suspicious how I would know an abbey has been founded on his land? What do I say? A wee lassie from the future told me Melrose Abbey was founded in 1290 on your land? I would be a laughing stock."

"Then you'll never know if she's telling the truth."

"Och, she can't be. It's not possible."

He wasn't as certain as his words sounded. Part of the reason he didn't want to check her story was he feared it might be true. If that was the case there was a chance she would go back to her time and he'd never see her again. He'd yearned for her the entire time they'd been patrolling and he couldn't imagine a time when he might never see her again.

When they reached the castle, he was glad to find her there. A fear had grown in him during the ride that she had escaped and he was relieved to see her looking up at him as he rode in. She looked exhausted. "You have been working too hard," he said as he stopped his horse next to her. "You should rest."

"There's too much to do before the frosts start. I haven't got time to rest."

"Rory," he called to the steward next to her. "Can you spare her for a couple of hours?"

"I reckon we can survive."

"Then climb up here, lassie."

"Up there? Why?"

"I want to reward you for your hard work." He held out a hand and after a second of thought she took it.

With a yank of his arm, he lifted her through the air, guiding her to land on the horse in front of him. "It felt very different last time I was on here," she said, glancing back over her shoulder.

He had a sudden urge to kiss her. Instead, he kicked the sides of his horse and turned her back toward the portcullis which remained open.

As he rode through, he noted the stone walls that guarded it. "The gates can't be pushed open with stone behind it," she said, seeing where he was looking. "And to burn the props they'd need to demolish that wall first and that would take some time."

"While we drop burning oil through the murder holes," he replied, nodding his approval.

"Where are we going anyway?" she asked as they began to move away from the castle.

"You'll see."

Chapter Ten

Beth wondered if he could tell she was trembling. It was the morning after Andrew's return to the castle and the first thing he'd done was send for her to join him in the courtyard.

She'd found him there on the back of his horse, holding out his hand to lift her up. A moment later she was sitting in front of him and they were riding out, the light of the dawn barely breaking over the horizon.

She had tried to tell him about the future as they rode, about how she would need to get back there sooner or later and find her mother. He had said nothing in response.

They turned off the main track about a mile from the castle slowly descending through a ravine, mountain peaks towering over them on both sides. The journey went on for a long time until they were far from the castle, the mountains shifting behind them, new ranges appearing on the horizon.

She told herself it was just the shade and the breeze making her cold but each time his hand moved on the reins of the horse, his arm brushed her side and her trembling intensified. Could he tell?

He still hadn't told her where they were going, only that it was a surprise. He had a slight smile on his face when he said it, a smile that she rarely saw. Most of the time he looked stern, angry even, and she could guess why.

He had a castle that needed rebuilding and he needed to find the money to pay for it. He had other clans constantly testing his defenses and he had the winter coming. She could imagine his worries. Was there enough food to feed everyone? Could they survive a siege? Would her work on the castle be done in time?

The ravine finally widened out as they reached the bottom of the slope, turning into a broad expanse of pasture. Sheep grazed on the grass around them as they made their way toward a wide expanse of water.

"How are we going to cross that?" she asked. "I see no bridge nor boat."

"We are not crossing it. We are going to swim in it."

"Swim? In that?"

"Aye. You sound surprised. Can you not swim?"

"I can swim but it'll be freezing."

"You'll see." He turned the horse and they followed the edge of the loch, coming out of the shadow of the mountain into sunlight once more.

The spot he had chosen was completely hidden from view. Only when they were on top of it did she realize what she was looking at. A tiny stream of water led from the loch to a circular pool of water that was a mere fairy pond, no more than twenty feet from side to side.

It was surrounded by broad armed trees and through their leaves, the sunlight sparkled on the water. To the far side were tall rocks that looked as if they'd fallen from the mountain many years before. They were covered in moss and between them a rivulet of water trickled down into the pool.

"What do you think?" Andrew asked, climbing down from the horse and holding a hand out to her.

"I think it looks beautiful," she replied, accepting his offer of help.

As she slid from the horse, he took her by the waist, lifting her down gently to the ground. His hands remained on her for a brief moment before he stepped away, dipping his hand into the water of the pool, sending ripples across the surface. "Doesn't feel too cold to me."

He stood up and undid the tartan baldric across his shoulder, pulling it free and folding it neatly before laying it across a rock. "Coming in?" he asked, diving straight into the pool and disappearing from view.

Beth winced on his behalf, laughing when his head emerged a moment later. "Isn't it cold?"

"See for yourself."

"You expect me to jump in just like that?"

"Or you could sit on that rock and do nothing if you prefer."

She looked at him and then at the water. "All right but turn the other way. I don't want you watching me undress."

He nodded before swimming away from her. She glanced around her, suddenly feeling she was being watched from the mountains. She shook the feeling away, untying the barbette under her chin before pulling her hair free from under the filet.

She slid off her shoes, enjoying the feel of the soft grass under her feet as she lifted the dress up and over her head.

She stopped for a moment, trying to decide whether to keep the kirtle on. Then she reasoned that her bra and panties were no more revealing than a bikini on the beach. With a shrug and a whispered, "I can't believe I'm doing this," she pulled the kirtle off and lay it down next to the dress.

Seeing he'd reached the far end of the pool and was about to turn she ran to jump in, ducking under the water before he caught sight of her body.

She gasped as the cold hit her but within seconds her body grew used to it. The chattering of her teeth slowed and then stopped.

"What do you think?" Andrew asked, swimming across to her.

"It's wonderful," she replied, doggy paddling slowly toward him. "Just what I needed."

"You've been working too hard," he said. "You need to relax now and then."

"Says you. I don't think I've seen you relax once."

"I'm doing it now, am I not?"

"I suppose so."

She caught sight of something out the corner of her eye but when she looked behind her, there was only a sheep nuzzling at her kirtle. "Leave that alone," she shouted.

Andrew laughed. "What is that you're wearing?"

She looked down and blushed as she realized the water was crystal clear, revealing her bra and panties. "My underwear," she said, turning away. "And I'll thank you not to look."

"What is that thing around your chest?"

"A bra. You've seen bras before, haven't you?"

"Only of cloth. Yours looks like nothing I've ever known. And you wear the smallest thing between your legs. Is that the fashion for ladies now?"

"It is where I come from. Now are we swimming or are you still gawping at me?"

"I dinnae ken why I cannae do both."

She splashed water at him, a mock scowl on her face. Inside she could feel herself relaxing, the tension of the day fading away. She knew she should feel more shy but something about being with Andrew made her feel totally at ease.

She knew with absolute certainty that she was safe by his side, that he would do nothing to hurt her despite his enormous bulk and the hungry way he was suddenly looking at her.

"What?" she asked. "What is it?"

He swam over to her, taking hold of her hands and pulling her over to the side of the pool. Leaning back against a low hanging willow branch, he smiled. "I have something I need to tell you."

She knew what was coming. He was going to tell her she wasn't good enough for him, that her days as master mason were over. She winced, ready for the worst.

"I want you to stay," he said, his face deadly serious.

She leaned against the branch next to him, turning to look more closely at him. "What, here in the pool?"

"Och, dinnae talk daft. I mean in my castle with me for good."

"I...I can't do that."

"Jings, woman. Why ever not? Where else would you go?"

"I've told you. I need to get back to my own time. I need to find my mom. She needs me. I'm only staying long enough to get the work on the go."

"I thought you'd given up on that nonsense. You know as well as I do that this is your time as much as its mine. There's no portal to the future in the old hall. There's nothing but wood and stone there."

"Are you calling me a liar?"

"No," he said, taking her hand in his. "I think you sincerely believe what you're saying is true but…" His voice tapered off into nothing.

"But what?"

"But even if it's true, I still want you to stay."

"I can't. Don't you understand I can't?"

"But you've done so much for my castle. Don't you want to see it finished?"

"Is that what you care about? The castle?"

"No, that isnae it at all."

She noticed his hand gripping her tighter. He pulled her towards him through the water, his face inches from hers. "What is it then?" she asked, holding her breath as he leaned ever closer.

"I want you to stay because I want you," he said, kissing her a second later.

His lips brushed over hers and he almost moved away but then he pressed more firmly, embracing her with his eyes closed.

Beth was too shocked to move at first but then the tingling from her lips moved through her body and she knew at once this was right. She could never have described how she knew to anyone but she knew.

It was a kiss like none she'd ever experienced, bringing her to life, her heart thudding even as she felt more relaxed than she ever had before. She melted into his arms as he threw his hands around her back, drawing her closer.

She could feel his body against her as their embrace grew stronger. Then all of a sudden he pulled his head away, her lips feeling his absence almost as strongly as they'd felt the kiss. "What?" she asked. "What's wrong?"

"Did you hear that?"

"Hear what?" she asked.

"Hush," he whispered, swimming quickly to the far side of the pool. All she could hear were a few rocks rolling down the mountainside far away.

He stuck his head out, peering into the distance before returning to her, the smile gone from his face as if it had never been there. "We must hide," he said. "There is a band coming this way."

"Hide? Hide where?"

"Behind the trees. There's a gap just there. Come, quiet as you can. They're wearing our tartan but I recognize none of their faces. There is something about this I dinnae like." He helped her out of the pool and she shivered in the cold as together they squeezed between the thick tree trunks.

Andrew glanced out before ducking back, his face pale. "I've an awful bad feeling about this," he whispered. "We must just hope they haven't seen us."

"Our clothes," she hissed but it was too late. From the ravine a voice called out. "Down there."

"I must go for my sword," Andrew said, darting out from between the trees. "Stay hidden no matter what happens."

Then he was gone and she was alone.

Chapter Eleven

Derek sat in his chamber, his face lit only by the single candle on the table in front of him. A rivulet of wax was running slowly downward from the flickering flame. He watched its progress, his eyes narrowed, his fingers neatly folded under his chin.

The fire had gone out. He didn't care. He didn't notice how cold the room had become. All he wanted to think about was the candle. Nothing else. Not until word came back that it was done.

He was going to be responsible for a laird's death. It was a big risk he was taking and he could only pray it would work out.

He took slow steady breaths, in and out, trying to keep calm. Soon he would need to appear shocked and he wanted it to seem as natural as possible. How best to be surprised?

"The laird's been kidnapped? Oh no, how awful."

"Dead you say?"

"I can't believe it. How?"

He tried to twist his face into despair, doing his best to make himself cry. No tears came. It wasn't easy acting shocked when he didn't know if the plan would work or not.

He looked at the quill pen laid on the table beside the candle. Such a simple little thing, he thought, picking it up and examining the drop of ink still left at the tip. He could use it to send another letter to his father, only to have it ignored once again. Or he could use the same pen to hire a bunch of mercenaries to kidnap a laird. Many things could be achieved by the sweep of a quill upon parchment.

It was all Andrew's fault. Not least because he'd taught Derek to read and write. If he hadn't, Derek would have been unable to write the letter. The thought was amusing in many ways.

The letter had gone out a few days earlier to those he'd hired to burn the hall. It made clear that it would be in their interest to be at the clearing near the stone circle twelve miles north-west of MacLeish castle. Derek had ridden out early, hoping that Andrew wouldn't return before he got back. That would ruin his carefully thought out plans.

Burning him in the old hall had not worked. How was he to know Rory would call Andrew back to the castle at the last minute?

This time he hoped things would work out better. The candle began to splutter. Still he did not move. He kept staring and breathing slowly, waiting to hear one way or another.

The rest of the castle had been too busy working on Beth's building scheme to notice when he went to the stone circle.

She was part of the reason he had written the letter in the first place. All the careful attention he had paid to the castle's flaws ready for the assault and she was merrily fixing them all. That fact had forced his hand before he was ready.

When Andrew had refused to be inside the old hall to burn to death his first thought was a full frontal assault. He had suggested as much to his father but had been told in no uncertain terms that the truce would not be broken unless they could guarantee an easy victory.

At first he thought the flaws in the defenses would be enough but then he thought about Andrew's routine, how he always went swimming after a long ride. That was when he thought just how his father would be able to guarantee the easy victory he wanted.

Derek met the mercenaries in the clearing. At their front was their leader, Rufus Longshanks, a scarred immensely tall villain who would sell his own grandmother to the Normans if the purse was heavy enough to make it worth his while.

"You offer me half a pound of silver for this?" he said when Derek arrived, waving his letter back at him. "It's not enough. You have yet to pay us for the fire. I want a pound."

"You would have got a pound if he'd died in the fire like he was supposed to but you didn't think to check first, did you?"

"How were we to know he wasn't in the building? You swore he'd be there. We did everything you asked of us."

"I didn't ask you to burn the houses. Why did you do that?"

Rufus shrugged. "He showed no sign of coming after us. Why didn't he chase us so we could kill him out of sight like you said?"

Derek felt his temper rising but he managed to bite down on it. "I was sure he'd chase the MacLeish tartan into that trap," he snapped. "That was not my fault."

"We sat in that wood waiting for him, swords and rope ready, like you said."

"Look, forget about that. How much did you make last year?" he asked, walking over to the altar and lifting himself onto it, sitting facing the men.

"A quarter of a pound almost. Why?"

"Because if you'd done your job you've have had half a pound by now."

"We did our job."

"I'm not arguing with you. As it is, I have a chance for you to redeem yourself. Half a pound for one night's work."

"Kidnapping a laird is not easy if he will not come to us. How are we supposed to get into the castle and get him out?"

"Who said anything about you getting into the castle?"

"How do we get him then?"

"Every time he comes back from patrols he goes swimming and I know where. All you have to do is watch and wait and then take him while his guard's down. There won't even be a fight unless he's started swimming with his sword at his hip."

Rufus smiled a toothless grin. "Now we're talking. All he's done to cut down on outlaws. We can barely make a living anymore. Where does he swim?"

"We have a deal then?"

One of the other men stepped forward, his eyes darting from left to right, never still for a moment. "I dinnae trust this one," he said. "Come, Rufus, let's away before we are hanged for this treachery."

"I brought no one with me," Derek replied. "You could kill me now and no one would be any the wiser."

"Then let's do it," the man said, drawing his sword.

"Only then you won't get your half pound of silver." Derek brushed a piece of dirt from the knee of his hose. "I only pay once the job's done. Do we have a deal?"

"Aye," Rufus replied. "And you better pay up or my sword may have two more notches on the handle by week's end.

Derek had cause to remember that conversation as he sat up in the tower. He had to steal from the treasury to make sure he had enough money to pay for it. That worried him more than murder. No one could link him to Andrew's death but someone might find the silver before he could pay the mercenaries.

Andrew had to die. Derek had tried to persuade him to unite with the MacLeishes against the English but the stubborn fool would hear nothing of it.

"Only when they stop stealing from us," was his reply every time as if life were that black and white. "Until then Duff MacLeish may be your father but he is not my ally."

Derek knew life wasn't black and white. It was all kinds of shades of gray.

Was he good or bad? He wanted Andrew dead and the clans united so they could defend the highlands against the English. Did that make him good or bad?

What about hiring the mercenaries to burn the hall while wearing MacLeish tartan? Was that the work of a villain or a cunning hero?

What about stealing the money to pay them? He had taken the half a pound of silver out of the treasury. That was theft which was bad. But it was to help secure the highlands which was good.

The silver would pay the mercenaries. The mercenaries would kill Andrew. With him out of the picture, Derek would send for his father to take over MacIntyre castle.

The clans would unite. He would finally get the acclaim he deserved and best of all, no one important would get hurt. Except the Normans who when they finally attacked would be sent back to England with arrows sticking out of their arses. Surely that made him a hero even if he had to get his hands a bit dirty to get it all done.

He could picture his father sitting in the hall at MacLeish castle, nodding to him. "Well done, my son. You are welcome to come home where you belong. You have proved yourself a man and a MacLeish. I am proud of you, my boy. Forgive me for sending you away."

The thought made him smile. It was all he'd ever wanted, praise from his father. It had never happened in his lifetime. He'd had more kind words from Andrew than he'd ever had from Duff yet they meant nothing coming from a MacIntyre.

The candle went out, the light dying away in the chamber. He stood up and crossed to the window. Was it done yet? Was Andrew already dead? When would the message come?

All he could do was wait. When Andrew had ridden into the castle after his patrols, he had gone off swimming the next morning in that utterly predictable way of his. Derek didn't need to see him go. He made sure lots of people saw him working hard, guaranteeing him an alibi should it be needed. Rufus and his men would be waiting on the mountainside, watching for his arrival.

It was only later in the day that he heard she'd gone with him. That didn't change the plan. Perhaps they'd kill her as well. It wasn't just because she'd rejected his advances, slapping him across the face just because she knew she was under Andrew's protection and he could not punish her like she deserved. It was because she was acting more like a laird every day, telling people what to do, getting Rory under her thumb, the steward following her every command.

What if the mercenaries took her for ransom? They weren't being paid to do so but maybe they'd use her to try and get more silver out of him. Fat chance. They could keep her as far as he was concerned. And what was left in the treasury would be his to use soon enough. No money wasted on rebuilding an old hall. It would go on feasts and clothes like it was supposed to. What was the point of storing wealth and never using it? Andrew went round in that old baldric. When he was in charge he'd have furs and silks like a proper noble. He'd give feasts the like of which the highlands had never seen before.

The first feast would be for his father. Duff would give him whatever he wanted for doing this and what he wanted was MacIntyre castle. He'd become laird in all but name. He'd make the rules for a change. He'd waited long enough, being forced to serve the chief of a rival clan for years on end, unable to leave, unable to make any decisions for himself. He'd had enough of servitude.

He began to pace the room in the darkness, feeling tension rising inside him. He should have had word by now. It had been hours since Andrew had gone.

They were supposed to send a message straight to the castle once it was done. He was ready, poised to take over. He had his letter ready to send to his father. Duff might have ignored the last one but he wouldn't ignore one telling him MacIntyre castle was his for the taking.

That letter sat sealed in the locked wall safe, the only key in his pocket. The moment word came, he would send a messenger with the letter and then it would all be over.

No longer would he be the servant. He'd be the master. Maybe even take Beth as his wife if she did make it back. She was pretty enough even if she did act too like a man for his liking. She'd have to stop all that master mason nonsense.

There'd be no time for taking a man's job when she'd have babies to sire and then raise. That was what MacLeish women were supposed to do. How come no one else seemed to care?

He stared out of the window, ignoring the cold wind hitting his face. The torches on the walls being rebuilt made it impossible to see beyond. He couldn't tell if anyone was heading for the castle. Hopefully word would come soon.

If it happened quickly enough, the MacLeishes would not need to attack at all. He could get the portcullis to stay open by cutting the ropes while the MacIntyres were still deciding what to do about an oncoming army. They could be taken without a siege and it would all be because of him.

He should be happy about it. Yet when he heard the sound of the portcullis being raised out in the courtyard he didn't feel happy. He felt an odd sense of dread.

He ran down the stairs in time to find a horse riding in at full gallop. On its back was no messenger. Holding the reins was Beth and in front of her, slumped in her arms, was the unconscious and badly bleeding body of Andrew MacIntyre.

Chapter Twelve

Beth could barely keep her eyes open. She blinked the blood away, looking up and sighing with relief as she saw the scaffolding of the keep in front of her. They had made it. She had no idea how.

In front of her, Andrew was moving again but only just. She had somehow managed to keep him on the horse as they'd made their frantic dash for the castle. She was glad the horse knew the way home, even with a gash in its side. All she'd had to do was hold on.

"What happened?" a voice was asking and she had to stare hard to be able to focus, her vision blurring as she slid from the horse and fell to the ground. She pushed herself upright, blinking again and seeing Derek's worried face peering back at her. "What happened?" he asked again.

"We were attacked," she replied. "You must get him to the infirmary. He needs help."

A bell was already ringing somewhere. Wiping her face, Beth felt nausea wash over her. A flash of screaming faces ran through her mind. She was back by the lake again. There were six of them and from her vantage point she saw far more than she ever wanted to of the ensuing battle. So much blood.

"What happened?" another voice asked.

"James," Derek said, grabbing the other man by the arm. "Andrew's been hurt. Help me get him into the infirmary. Tell the blacksmith the horse needs looking at too. Beth, can you walk?"

"Yes," she said, her voice coming from far away. The bells faded and her eyes closed again.

She was back in the clearing by the lake. Everything happening so slowly. She wanted to cry out but she couldn't say anything as she relived the attack.

Andrew grabbed his sword and was swinging it at the men. They tried to encircle him but he had his back to the pool and they had no idea how deep it was. With a slash of the blade, he caught one on the arm as he advanced, sending him stumbling away. Two more plunged forward, jabbing and slicing him open at the shoulder and on the thigh.

She couldn't stay hidden. She ran out, picking up a rock as she went and hurling it at the attacking group. It caught one of them completely off guard, blood spraying from his nose as he fell back.

The others came on but Andrew was ready for them. The sound of swords clashing made her ears ring. She picked up another stone and threw it past Andrew at the last attacker.

He was proving hardest to defeat. The others were laid on the ground moaning, none of them in a fit state to carry on fighting. Andrew had fallen back into the water, visibly tiring, blood pouring down his face from a gash to the forehead.

Beth sprinted forward, picking up a sword as she went. She had no idea what she intended to do. She could barely lift the thing and as she swung it blindly toward the attacker, he twisted, catching her on the top of the head with his own blade. She ducked just in time but blood poured into her eyes nonetheless, making it impossible to see.

As she wiped it away she saw in freeze frame what was happening. Her failed attack had distracted the aggressor and Andrew had been able to hurl the tip of his sword forward, catching his opponent in the chest. The sword ran deep as the man's legs buckled.

He fell but as he did so, he turned and looked right at Beth, his eyes wide. "You're next," he said, his voice echoing around the valley. Suddenly he was standing over her, his sword high over his head, Andrew nowhere to be seen.

She sat bolt upright in bed, her eyes wild, looking about her for the sword. It took several seconds for her to realize where she was. The attacker hadn't risen from the dead. He hadn't spoken to her. It was a dream.

She was in the infirmary. The place was lit by candles and she could see only shadows moving beyond the glow. People were talking in low voices but they were too far away for her to make out what they were saying.

"Where is he?" she called out. "Where's Andrew?"

"Shush," a voice said and then James and Derek were at her side. "Try and rest."

"Oh God, he's dead isn't he?"

"No, lass," James said, lifting a horn cup to her lips. "He'll live. Here, drink this."

"What is it?"

"It's to calm your nerves. Crushed yarrow."

She took a sip and winced. "It tastes awful."

"Does you good though. Helps stop the bleeding too."

"Only when applied to the skin," said a new voice. "Don't you know anything, James?"

Beth turned to the source of the voice. It came from a figure standing in the doorway behind the other two men. "Andrew!" she shouted. "You're alive."

"Aye, thanks to you." He limped over to her, sitting on the edge of the bed. "How are you feeling?"

"Never mind me. What about you?"

He was covered in bandages, dried blood still covering his leg and half his face. "I'll live," he said, taking her hand in his. "Where did you learn to throw so well?"

"Baseball practise when I was about twelve."

"Baseball?"

"It's…never mind. I'll tell you some other time."

"I'll hold you to that."

"Who were they? I didn't get chance to ask on the way back because…"

"Because I was unconscious, I know. I thank you once again for getting us back to the castle."

"You must be more cautious," James said, lifting the bandage to examine the wound on Andrew's forehead. "Someone is out to get you."

"Any idea who it was?" Derek asked.

"They did not wear tartan but I suspect MacLeish had something to do with this."

"MacLeish?" Derek sounded shocked. "But why would we…I mean why would they?"

"I'm going to go and ask him myself. I will get the men together. Derek, you should come with us."

"Are you sure you don't want me to stay here and keep an eye on Beth? What if they attack while you're away?"

"I suppose you're right. I'll be back as soon as I can." He squeezed Beth's hand. "Rest a while."

"Must you go?" she asked. "You've lost a lot of blood. Surely you should rest too."

"I have to speak to Duff MacLeish first. If he's behind this he won't be expecting me to show up apart from as a bloodied corpse. The look on his face when I arrive unannounced at his castle will be all the answer I need as to his part in all this."

He turned and left with James and Derek. Beth sank back onto the bed. She wanted to sleep but every time she closed her eyes she was back in the clearing, swords slicing into flesh, men screaming in agony, Andrew's eyes lit up with a fire and brutality she never expected to see in him.

She found herself thinking about home, about a warm comfortable bed that wasn't stuffed with straw, where the risk of death wasn't around every corner.

All they'd done was go for a swim and they'd both almost died. What was worse, there was little chance of justice. There was no forensic team heading off to examine the scene. The men, if any survived, would have melted into the night. What was worse was they might come back anytime.

She tried once more to sleep but again the screams came into her head, echoing around her skull. She got up in the end, walking out of the infirmary to find Derek leaning against the wall in the courtyard as if he'd been waiting for her to emerge.

"Where are you going?" he asked, wagging a finger at her.

"I just want to go home," she replied. "I'll be safe at home."

He looked happier all of a sudden. "And where is home?"

"The hall at Pluscarden."

"You live at Pluscarden? Then why did none of the villagers recognize you?"

"Can you take me there?" she asked, feeling exhausted, her limbs heavy as if lead weights had been strapped to her wrists. "I can't stay here. It's too violent."

"Is it any safer at Pluscarden?"

"Will you stop me going?"

"On the contrary. Though I cannot take you myself, I can have someone show you the way."

"You would do that for me?"

"Aye."

"Thank you."

"Wait here." He crossed the courtyard and vanished into the keep.

While he was gone, Beth paced back and forth, trying to wake her exhausted limbs. A headache was building behind her eyes. She needed rest and she wasn't going to get it here. She just hoped when she got home the images of the battle would vanish along with her memories of this place.

She didn't want to remember it anymore. She had been mad to think she could stay at all. Andrew was a violent man in a violent world and he fitted in right at home swinging a sword about. She'd just thrown a couple of stones and it was enough to make her feel ill.

Besides, she should get back to her mother, look after her like she was supposed to, not leave her to fend for herself. She tried not to think about leaving Andrew behind. The thought of being without him did something deep inside her, opened a void that threatened to swallow her whole if she gave it as much as a moment's thought.

Get home, she told herself. What happens here is nothing to do with me. It all took place hundreds of years ago if I look at it properly and I shouldn't be getting involved at all. Butterfly effect and all that.

She looked up at the walls, seeing the scaffolding that was only in place because of her. She had already changed the future. The place would be far stronger when it was done. She would be sorry not to see the end of the work but this was the right thing to do.

"Are you ready?" Derek asked, sneaking up on her from nowhere. "Meet Rufus. He was just on his way out and he's agreed to take you back to Pluscarden." He nodded to the other man. "Isn't that right Rufus?"

"Aye," the mountain of a man next to Derek said, dark eyes all that were visible from under his even darker hood. "Come on, lassie. Let's get going."

Chapter Thirteen

It was a route Andrew knew well. Ancient and covered in scars, it reminded him of himself. He was as worn out and damaged by all this conflict as the road they traveled along. Even the rain sensed his mood, growing heavier the further they traveled, soaking the men and their horses.

Beth had mentioned rebuilding the roads and the system she'd described made sense but what was the point when the road itself crossed into MacLeish land. Was he supposed to patch up their land as well as his own? If not, there was little point in his tracks draining better if the horses only had to stumble along once more when they reached the borders.

The ride from the castle took them north, first passing by the ruins of Pluscarden and the old hall. The new building was coming along but he noticed the window in what would become the bedchamber was in the wrong place. It was supposed to be further to the left. He'd have to have a word with the laborers on the way back. Now was not the time to get involved in the master mason's job.

He knew mistakes were the price of keeping Beth back in the castle but look what happened when he let her out last time. The two of them had almost been killed. She was safest there.

The faces of those who attacked were seared into his brain. If he ever saw them again, he would deal with them properly. They were ill trained and poorly fed, that was the only reason why he'd been able to win. Six of them and yet none fit to wield a sword. Were they all dead? He could only hope so.

It made him nervous to wonder if anyone more competent might be out there. He was taking a risk riding to MacLeish castle but it had to be done. What would it say about a laird if he was too afraid to ride out from his own castle?

He had only brought Gillis, Finley, and Wallace with him. Given how high tempers had risen the last time he'd seen Duff MacLeish, he wanted to do nothing to raise suspicions on this foray.

The road eased left after Pluscarden, taking a lazy path between fields of oats until it reached the great wood at the foot of Am Basteir. The mountain was a jagged lump of gray rock that seemed to point an accusing finger at the sky. He remembered climbing to the top of that peak when he was twelve, proving to the clan that he was worthy of being laird one day, pointing his finger at the sky.

He had stood on the top for two full days as storms raged around him. He well recalled the fear coursing through him that lightning might strike at any moment. It didn't of course, exactly as Fenella had foretold. He had climbed back down on the dawn of the third day, his arms aching, his body shaking from the cold and the hunger. Only then was he truly a MacIntyre.

He smiled as he recalled how scared he'd been by a bit of lightning. So different to the true horrors that were waiting for him when he came of age. A succession of images flashed through his head, one battle after another, his sword cleaving skulls, that mace strike that crushed his arm, rendering it useless for weeks. He'd only survived that thanks to Gillis coming to his aid.

Then he thought of the attack by the pool and he grimaced, staring into the distance but not seeing anything.

He thought of the kiss he'd shared with Beth, the hunger it had given rise to inside him. He had wanted more. Much, much more. The moment his lips pressed to hers, he wanted her in her entirety. He wanted her body, her mind, her soul. He felt as if part of her reached inside him and tugged at his heartstrings, wrapping around them and not letting go.

Poor Beth. She didn't deserve any of this. He felt a pang of anxiety at the thought of her laid back in her infirmary bed. At least she had Derek and James keeping an eye on her. She should be safe. If only the same could be said for him.

He had no idea what would happen at MacLeish castle but he needed to know the truth. Was Duff MacLeish trying to get him killed? It didn't make sense but it was the only possible explanation. Twice an attempt had been made on his life. The first time Duff had denied it and he'd believed him but for it to happen twice? That was too much for coincidence.

The attacks were unusual though, not MacLeish's usual style. They weren't Norman methods either. The English tended to come in force, provoking battle and attempting to overwhelm the highlanders with superior numbers.

It was only Andrew's intimate knowledge of the terrain that had kept them at bay so far. The southerners dared not fight among the mountains with so many hiding places for the clan to mount sneak attacks on their rearguard, picking them off one by one, weakening them enough to send them running for home with whispers of highland ghosts chasing after them.

The track descended into the valley for a couple of miles before climbing again, passing between two mountains and then coming to a cairn of stones beside the road. The end of MacIntyre land and the start of MacLeish territory.

It was only a single step forward and yet with it the risk increased tenfold. From here on in, the MacLeishes might attack at any time. Would they honor the peace accord or see the strategic advantage of taking Andrew when he only had three men with him?

He knew he was relying on a truce that had lasted well over a decade but had they not already broken it? He sat up straight and tall on his horse. If they were to come, let them come. He would fight with honor if it came to it. Could the same be said of them? God would judge them all in the end.

People looked at them as they rode past, glancing up from the fields, muttering to each other at the sight of MacIntyre tartan on their land. Andrew ignored them, staring straight ahead. He had a job to do and nothing would distract him.

Another hour and then they were there. An escort had appeared from nowhere, six gruff unspeaking MacLeish men at arms, riding three to the left and three to the right, keeping pace with them for the last few miles until they reached MacLeish castle.

The old keep was still standing inside the walls but next to it the broken walls of the new building were higher than when he last saw them, at least twenty feet and still rising. The sound of masons chiseling echoed out to them as they stopped by the drawbridge.

On the far side, the guard looked pale. He was no more than fifteen. Duff MacLeish was clearly not expecting anyone. Was that significant?

"Halt," the guard said in a squeaky voice.

"We already have," Finley shouted back. "Are you going to stand there dithering or are you going to inform your lord the laird of the MacIntyre clan is here to see him?"

"Let them in, Malcolm," one of the escort shouted. "Show some manners."

"Come in, my laird," Malcolm shouted, beckoning them over.

Andrew rode in through the gate, stopping in the courtyard and looking once more at the new keep.

"He looks like he's planning for quite the siege," Wallace said in a low voice. "Perhaps he is preparing for clan war after all."

"I doubt it," Gillis replied. "It'll be ten years before it's finished and until then all he has is children guarding his gates and that crumbling ruin to keep him safe."

"Andrew MacIntyre," a voice shouted from the doorway of the old keep. "Come inside."

Duff was waving them over. Andrew nodded to his men before dismounting. Stableboys ran over at once, guiding the steeds away. There was more pointing and whispering from MacLeish people as Andrew headed over to the keep. He glanced around, wondering if he might see any faces he recognized from his swim with Beth. No luck.

"What do you think of the new keep?" Duff asked when Andrew reached him.

"Planning a war?" Andrew asked.

There was a gasp from the stewards behind Duff but the MacLeish laird didn't rise to the bait. "You tell me," he said. "Come, let us break bread together before we start the bickering."

Once they were all seated in the hall around the long table, Duff tore a strip from the trencher in front of him, dipping it into a jug of gravy before chewing it slowly. Around him sat other MacLeishes, contempt visible on their faces as they stared at Andrew.

"What brings you here?" Duff asked when he was done with the ceremonial first bite. "You dinnae look so well."

Andrew chewed his own bread, thinking how best to word things. "I was attacked."

"That I can see. Who by?"

"I thought you might know."

Duff's brow furrowed. "Careful, laddie. That's the second time you've accused me of something recently. It's almost as if you want a clan war."

"I want peace, MacLeish. That's all I've ever wanted. And yet my people are burned and I barely escape death when half a dozen mercenaries attack me. I think you hired them and I think you should tell me why you're so desperate to get rid of me. I thought Derek was your peace offering to end our feuds."

"And I think you should leave," Duff said, getting to his feet, his voice cold. "If I were you I'd think hard before making any more accusations of this nature."

Andrew wasn't finished yet. "Are you telling me you had nothing to do with this?"

"I swear on the bones of my ancestors I dinnae have any idea what you're blathering about. Now be off with you laddie and dinnae come back unless it's with a peace offering of your own, not accusations with no proof beyond your own prejudice."

Andrew stood up, picking up the last of his bread and swallowing it as was the custom. "This isnae over," he said, turning and heading for the door.

Outside he stood in the rain a few feet from the new keep, looking up at it and the laborers still working despite the appalling conditions. "That was foolish," Gillis said, coming to stand next to him. "Antagonizing him was not a good idea."

"Aye, maybe you're right," Andrew replied. "I cannae help my anger when enemies appear around every corner. Where the blazes are the horses?"

"Coming," a boy's voice shouted, waving at them from the stables. "Sorry, my laird. Forgive me."

"He's no your laird," Duff shouted from the keep doorway. "He's an unwelcome guest and he's not welcome back until he learns some manners."

Andrew bowed theatrically to Duff before mounting his horse. "Come on," he said to his men. "Before we get arrows in our backs."

They rode swiftly out the gate, none of them breathing easy until they were back on their own territory. He blinked the rain from his eyes as they passed the cairn. In all that time none of his men had spoken a word. He himself was lost in thought. Was Duff telling the truth? Or was it all bluster to try and distract him?

Not for the first time he wished his father was still alive to consult. He wanted help deciding what to do next and neither of the potential options seemed ideal. Start a war or live in fear for the rest of his life.

As they rode past Pluscarden, Andrew noticed the window in the wrong place. He made a mental note to have a word with them about that. Not now though, he had too many other things to think about.

They were about five miles from the castle when he saw something in the corner of his eye. "Hold," he said, stopping his horse in the middle of the road.

"What is it?" Gillis asked, looking where he was staring.

It was hard to tell but in a wood to his left he'd seen something. He looked again. "I saw someone over there."

"Who? A verderer?"

"No. It looked like one of the men who attacked me. Wait there."

"Should we not come with you?"

"No, we all ride on until we're out of sight of the wood. Then I'll run back sneak up on him. You keep riding for the castle."

"Why not take him by force?"

"Because I want to take him alive if I can and having him think we've not seen him is the best way to do that. Now move before he notices."

They rode on until they were round the next bend. "Keep my horse moving," Andrew said as he jumped to the ground. "Try and shield it so he thinks I'm still riding with you."

"Be careful," Gillis said. "It could be a trap."

Andrew didn't answer, he was already moving off, crouching low, hiding behind the stalks of wheat. Was he being paranoid? What had he seen really? A momentary flash of a face before a figure vanished into the wood. Was that enough to send him crawling through the mud in the driving rain?

He kept moving forward. He had a bad feeling in the pit of his stomach. Something was wrong. He wanted to turn back but he didn't. Above his head thunder rumbled. A storm was coming.

Chapter Fourteen

Beth couldn't take any more. She'd been accused of burning down half a village. She'd been slapped. She'd been locked in a tower. She'd been almost killed in that loch. She'd seen people die. She'd been lied to so many times she'd lost count and somehow she hadn't learned her lesson. Now she was bound to a tree because she was too trusting.

Derek had told her she would be safe with Rufus, that he would guide her back to the old hall and protect her while she made her way home. What happened instead? Tied up with no way of escaping.

She tried once more to break free from the ropes holding her to the tree. He would be back soon. This might be her only chance.

At first the walk from the castle seemed fine. Her companion said nothing as they headed out along the road to Pluscarden but she hadn't minded that. Some of the servants were verbose, others saying nothing unless spoken to. He was obviously one of the latter type.

Then they reached the turn by the wood. He saw something he didn't like ahead of them. Without pausing, he grabbed her by the arm. "Hurry," he said. Bandits intent on bloodshed."

She trusted him. She had no reason not to. She caught a glimpse of horses on the road in the distance as they ran to the wood, soon hidden from view. That was when he'd revealed his face. "I know you," she said as he slid the hood backward.

"Aye, lassie. I ken you do."

She saw him laid on the ground by the loch. Had he just feigned death? "You tried to kill Andrew."

"And now I'm supposed to kill you but I'm not going to."

"You're not?" As she spoke she backed slowly away from him but he noticed within seconds, lunging for her and grabbing her wrist.

She fought to free herself but to no avail. Clawing at him did nothing. He just laughed as he pulled out a knife and pointed it toward her. "Sit yourself down there and dinnae move or I'll have to take out one of those pretty eyes of yours."

She considered running, then remembered how far they'd come from the castle. How many people had she seen? No more than half a dozen and all far away in the fields. The knife looked wickedly sharp and it was inches from her face. She didn't run.

Within a minute she was tied to the tree, sitting on the soaking wet earth, cold spreading through her, feeling once again that this world was not meant for her. What was happening just convinced her all the more that she needed to get home. It was too dangerous.

If she could just get out of the ropes, she could sneak away from him, hide deeper in the wood, wait until dark and then find her way to the old hall on her own.

The rain continued to drip on her through the foliage above, soaking the ropes. She tugged as hard as she could but he had tied her too tightly. Why hadn't she run? She thought of the knife, how easily it might cut into her and how no one would know.

No one knew where she was, not even Derek. He'd just sent her along the road. Did he know who his servant really was? A thought flashed through her mind. Had he done this as revenge for her slapping him when they first met?

Her captor had said he was going to check on the horses going past. Would they be close enough to hear her shout? Was it worth trying? She heard a twig snap and then he was back, knife still in his hand. "Good lass," he said, a cruel grin spreading across his face. "They've all gone by so time for us to be moving on."

"Where to?" she asked, not liking the way he was looking at her.

"You can come back to my camp with me, keep me company there. All we need is a horse to ease the journey and I'll have one stolen in two minutes. Don't go anywhere, will you?"

He laughed at his joke before he left her again, disappearing out of the trees, leaving her to continue her struggle with the bonds holding her in place.

Why had she let him tie her up? She should have run. It was better than the alternative, being taken to his camp and trapped with him.

There was a movement in front of her, something coming through the trees. Was he back already? Then a figure stepped out and Beth felt a huge wave of relief wash over her, warming her frozen bones. "Andrew!" she said. "Is it really you?"

"Aye, lassie," he replied, striding across to her. "Where is he?"

"He went that way, said he was going to steal a horse."

She looked up at him as he pulled out a knife. Before she had time to ask what he planned to do he was kneeling down and cutting through the ropes that tied her to the tree.

"Look out!" she cried, seeing past him as her captor returned, his dirk held high over his head.

He swung the blade down toward Andrew's unprotected neck but all it sliced was thin air. The laird rolled neatly to the right, flicking out his foot as he went, catching his attacker on the ankle and sending him sprawling into the wet mud.

Andrew roared, diving onto the outlaw, landing one punch after another. The two of them rolled together in the mud.

Beth tugged the last of the ropes away and got to her feet, unsure of what to do.

"Do you yield," Andrew asked, fist clenched above the other man's head.

The man nodded frantically, spitting out a blackened tooth. "Aye. Just dinnae hurt me no more."

Andrew stood up slowly, looking down at the stricken figure. "On your feet."

The man got up slowly but as he did so, he suddenly lunged forward, the dirk still in his hand. Beth went to shout a warning but Andrew had already reacted, leaping to one side and again sticking out a foot.

The man tripped over it, stumbling and falling onto his own blade. He landed heavily, gurgling as he did so. He writhed in place, rolling onto his back, the dirk sticking out of his chest.

"Who sent you?" Andrew asked, grabbing him by the neck. "Tell me who sent you and I'll stop the bleeding.

"Dirk," the man said, his fingers wrapping around the handle of the blade, trying to pull it out. "Dirk." It was the last thing he said, his eyes glazing over a second later.

Beth couldn't help it. Tears began to fall from her eyes. She'd seen too much death recently. It was more than she could take.

"Did he mention the MacLeishes?" Andrew asked, standing up and looking at her. "Why the sobbing, lassie? You're safe enough now."

"You think that's what matters? He's dead. You know before coming here I'd never seen a single dead body. It's all too much. I'm going home."

"Is that what you were doing out here? Were you trying to get back to the old hall?"

She nodded. "I couldn't even do that without someone else dying."

"You want to go back to your own time, don't you?"

She nodded before frowning. "Wait, are you saying you believe me?"

"Aye, lassie. I do."

"What made you change your mind?"

"You and your clothes and your knowledge of building techniques no one else has heard of. A stone vault for the hall, camber for the roads, all the rest at the castle. There's no other story that fits than the one you told from the start. Only..." His voice faded into nothing and he looked down at the ground between them.

"Only what?"

He looked up, straight into her eyes. He held out both his hands, swallowing hers. "I dinnae want you to go back."

She looked back at him, feeling his rough fingers on her own. "What? Why?"

"I want you to stay with me."

"But why? I don't understand why it matters so much to you."

"Because I love you."

Beth felt like she'd been punched in the stomach and lifted into the air at the same time. She was shocked beyond belief to hear those words. Sure, they'd shared a kiss but had he given any sign before that he loved her?

She realized something in that moment, something she'd always known when she looked deep inside herself, the reason why it had been so hard to go. "I love you too." At once a pang of guilt struck her. Her mother needed her.

"So you'll stay?"

Beth paused, thinking hard before answering. She looked down at the body on the ground next to them, knowing that staying might mean seeing many more like him. "I'll stay."

"I'm so glad you said that."

"But only until the building work is finished, then I must find my mother."

He nodded, his smile fading. "I understand."

He took her hand, leading her out of the wood to the fields beyond. The rain was slowing and in the distance a flash of blue sky appeared between the fast moving clouds. He stopped, planted his feet apart and grabbed her. "I dinnae know what sent you to me but I'm glad you came." Then he kissed her.

Beth felt a warmth spreading through her as they embraced but it was accompanied by a poignancy. How many more kisses would they get to share before she had to leave him forever?

Chapter Fifteen

Derek was seething. He sat with a smile fixed on his face, looking for all the world like he was glad to see Andrew and Beth were back in the castle.

The two of them sat together at the top table, eating dinner on that first night back in the great hall, the sounds of the clan echoing around the walls. Everyone was relieved the laird had survived. Derek cursed his misfortune. Three times he had arranged a foolproof plan to kill Andrew and thrice fate had stepped in his way.

He had been careful with his questions, gradually piecing together what had happened on this latest occasion. Take her into the woods. That part went as planned. With her out of the way he could easily get Andrew alone in the wood. Then help Rufus kill him. It should have been easy but he had to go and get himself killed.

Rufus had let him down for the third and last time. Dead he might be and with no way of confessing Derek's part in things but that still left the problem of Andrew to resolve. How to kill him?

One thing was for sure, he would not rely on anyone else again. He would find a way to do it himself. But how?

When they made jokes he laughed with the crowd but he offered none of his own. Instead, he sat silently making plans to solve his problems once and for all. He needed something that could not fail, something that didn't involve men like Rufus.

Andrew called for more ale, nodding a greeting to Derek when he saw him looking over at him. It was bad enough that all his plans had failed so far, to see that failure right in front of him was more than he could bear.

He stood up, excusing himself quietly before leaving, heading down to the courtyard to think alone in the cool night air.

He heard footsteps behind him in the mud less than a minute later. Turning he saw Andrew walking toward him. He managed to get the smile back on his face though it took all of his internal effort. "Not hungry, my friend?" Andrew asked, walking over to him.

"Stomach pain," he replied. "I was going to see James, see if he had some mint or chamomile."

"Before you go, do you have a moment?"

"Of course, my laird."

"Beth mentioned a couple of things to me today."

"I was so shocked to hear what happened to her. It sounded awful. How is she?"

The distraction didn't work. Andrew spoke quietly with no hint of emotion to his voice. Derek didn't like hearing him like that. Was he suspicious? "She said you helped her leave. Why was that?"

Derek had his answer already prepared. "She was desperate to go see the old hall. She told me she wanted to see how the building work was going on. I couldn't see the harm in it."

"Even though I told you to keep her safe here."

"Aye but I thought she'd be there and back before your return. She wouldn't keep blathering on about it and you'd be none the wiser. How could I have known what would happen?"

"You provided her guide, she said. Who was he?"

"You'll think me foolish but I showed pity on the villain. Said he was a beggar down on his luck. I offered him a groat to take her to the hall."

"Why?"

"He didn't want charity, he wanted work. I thought that was the best way to help them both. He seemed a decent enough man, I thought he'd keep her safe on the way there."

"I see. Well I won't keep you if you're stomach is bothering you. Off you go to James."

Derek could have laughed as he walked away. Andrew was so stupid. A few well placed words and it was all back to normal. He had gotten away with it.

The joy he felt was soon replaced by anger again. If he was to get hold of the castle he needed rid of that man but how best to do it?

He was no closer to a solution a fortnight later. In that time he had been forced to watch as the last of the work was completed on the chapel. All efforts had been focused on it, the battlements and the keep too big a job to get done before the winter. They had been covered over with cloth weighed down with stone to protect the mortar from frost over winter.

Beth had brought all the laborers together to get the roof of the chapel completed in time for the visit from the bishop. She was hoping to have the last of the work done in time for a service of blessing on the coming Sunday.

He stood in the courtyard watching the carpenters at work on the lengths of wood needed to support the roof. How had she become such an integral part of the clan in such a short space of time? He had been here fifteen years and still felt like an interloper.

All he wanted was to be welcomed back into the MacLeishes, accepted by his father. It would happen if only he could come up with a foolproof plan for getting rid of Andrew or taking over the castle. Or better still, achieving both at once.

Beth was talking to some of the workers and he tuned into the conversation, hoping to hear something to his advantage. It had been all he'd been able to do since their return, eavesdrop on them both. For the first time he realized she was saying something he might be able to make work. If only he could put the pieces together. An idea began to form in his head as she spoke.

"We cannot take the falsework down until the mortar is set."

The man she was talking to was nodding his head though he clearly disagreed. "It will look awful for the bishop with the falsework still in place. I think it's already set. It's had longer than any of the previous."

"In this cold it will take far longer to set than the last lot."

"Why don't we test it before he comes? Think how glorious it would look if he came and saw the chapel completed, the ceiling vaulted and the paint gleaming."

"I don't dispute that but it must be set first if we don't want it to collapse."

The idea took shape in Derek's mind and he walked away smiling. He didn't need to hear anymore.

That night he joined in the laughter at dinner with the rest, thinking how none of them knew what he had planned. They would soon find out. When he sat at the chair in the middle of the top table as laird of the castle they would know what he'd done but by then it would be too late. He'd be in charge.

That night he thought through his plan in detail. There were many things that might scupper it. All he could do was trust in God and himself and pray that it would work out for the best. After all, he had everyone's best interests at heart.

Get rid of Andrew. Then unite the clans and take on the English. If he was given the castle as his reward then that was just a piece of extra luck that he wouldn't turn down.

He pictured himself in Andrew's place. The feasts they would have, the changes he would make. It would all be very different under his regime. He shook the thoughts from his head. That was for the future. What he needed to concentrate on was making sure his plan worked.

On the Sunday the bishop was due to arrive the castle was frantic with activity. Fresh rushes had been laid in the hall and in the courtyard itself, forming makeshift paths through the mud. The livestock had been tidied away to pens outside the wall, everyone was in their best clothes in preparation for his arrival.

It was so busy no one noticed Derek sneaking into the chapel. The work had finished two days ago but the falsework was still in place. Derek looked up at it. Even he had to admit that she'd done a good job. The springers aligned perfectly on top of the new pillars. The voussoirs were ashlar and perfectly white and the keystones on top were intricately colored in red and white.

There was no chapel like it in all of Scotland. The vault of the ceiling would look perfect once the wooden falsework holding it up was removed.

The mortar had not set and so the bishop was just going to have to imagine how it would look once finished. Derek had other plans. He fetched a ladder from the back of the chapel and climbed up, taking down the first piece of falsework.

As it came out the stones shifted ever so slightly above his head before settling. Perhaps the mortar would be strong enough to survive after all. If that was the case then all his planning would be for nought.

It would work, he told himself as he moved the ladder to collect the next piece of falsework. The ceiling would collapse on Andrew. He could already hear it groaning above his head. He smiled as he took the rest of the falsework out, gathering what he could under his arm and carrying it out of the chapel.

It took three trips to get it all but the rushing about and hectic work around him played into his hands. No one noticed one more body carrying armfuls of things around. He dumped the wood around the back of the chapel, throwing rushes over the top to hide the falsework from view.

Stage one was done. The bishop was due any minute and then the chapel would be filled with people ready for the blessing. There was only one more part of his plan to put into action and it was walking straight toward the chapel at that very moment.

Andrew and Beth were rarely seen apart anymore. There was already talk of a possible future wedding. Derek didn't join in with the gossip. He knew for certain there would be no wedding because soon there would be no Andrew.

He ran over to them at the front of the group heading for the chapel. "Beth," he said. "Thank goodness I found you. I need a word."

"Can it not wait?" Andrew said. "The bishop has just arrived."

"There's a crack in the outer wall," he replied. "I thought you should know."

"What?" Beth asked. "Where?"

"This way."

She turned to Andrew. "You go on ahead. I'll be in as soon as I can."

Derek smiled to himself. If she'd gone into the chapel with the others she'd see at once that the falsework was no longer supporting the stone roof. With her out of the way everyone else would assume the mortar was set and that she'd made the decision at the last minute.

All he needed was to keep her out of the way, long enough for Andrew to get inside. It wouldn't be more than a few minutes before the roof collapsed on his head.

He headed out of the castle gateway just as the horns were blown to signal the bishop's arrival. "Where's the crack?" Beth asked as they headed down into the earthworks to look up at the towering battlements. "How serious is it?"

"Further round the corner," Derek replied, beckoning her on.

He thought about the chapel, about Andrew standing by the altar at that very moment. Then he thought of all the others in there too. Most of the castle would attend the service, packing the place full, all eager to hear the blessing of the bishop. They would all be killed too.

He felt a sudden lurch in his stomach. He'd been so focused on getting rid of Andrew that he hadn't even considered that. All the old people, the children too. They'd all be in there. And then there was the bishop. What if the bishop died?

Would he go to hell for causing the death of one of God's own men? The thought made him fear for his soul. He'd made a mistake. He shouldn't have done it.

"Are we there yet?" Beth asked as he stopped dead.

"Aye," he replied quietly, his mind elsewhere.

"I see no crack," she said, squinting as she looked up. "Are you sure it was here."

"Aye," he said again, barely listening. It was too late to do anything about the chapel. If he told them all to leave they'd know he was the one who removed the falsework. They'd ask why and he could think of no plausible explanation other than the truth.

Then he heard another set of horns. If the bishop had already arrived who was that being heralded? He looked up at the path leading to the castle gateway, his heart leaping into his mouth. It was his father and retinue.

"I'm going back to the service," Beth was saying but her voice came from far away. Had his father come to see the chapel being blessed? Was he about to kill his own pa alongside Andrew?

"Are you coming?"

He didn't move.

"I'll see you in there then." She walked away, leaving him frozen to the spot in the earthworks, with no earthly idea what to do.

Chapter Sixteen

"Sin by inaction is as venal as sin by action in the eyes of the Lord."

The bishop's voice boomed out from the front of the chapel, loud enough for Beth to hear him from outside. She wanted to be in there, standing beside Andrew but there was no chance. The place was absolutely packed. Not only were most of the clan inside but two dozen MacLeishes had turned up and space had somehow been made for them but it took all the room there was to do it.

She had left Derek in the earthworks looking up at the castle walls. There was something odd in his manner and she was glad to be away from him. She had never fully trusted him since he slapped her that time in the tower and he had behaved particularly oddly the last couple of weeks.

Andrew had told her what he'd said about the beggar guiding her to the old hall but she had her own suspicions. After all, the words of the dying man had sounded like "Dirk," which could have referred to the knife sticking out of him but could just as easily have been the word Derek.

She tried to put him out of her mind, taking a step back to admire the chapel. It had been a labor of love, taking up almost every waking hour as she'd wanted to get it just right for the bishop's visit. Something told her this was the reason why she'd come back in time. God had a purpose for her and this was it. She had completed a new chapel and she had done it in time for the bishop's visit.

He had originally been coming to check on the progress but with some quick calculations she realized it might be possible to finish it in time for his visit.

Sure, the mortar hadn't set and the roof was still a work in progress but what the eye didn't see, the master mason got away with. He wouldn't mind the falsework anyway, he would understand that mortar wasn't something you could will into setting. It took time but once it was done, if done right, it would last for centuries.

She thought of the old hall before the fire. She'd stood under her own vaulting work in the future and that had looked as good as on the day it was built.

The bishop was still talking. "Those that by their own inaction allow pain and suffering are as guilty in the Lord's eyes as those who inflict it by their action.

Inaction would have left the old chapel standing but we stand today under this superb vault, glorying God above man with its simple grandeur and as I look up at the vault there is nothing between it and us, nothing between our prayers and God himself."

Nothing but the falsework, Beth thought, trying once more to squeeze through the crowd in the doorway, hoping for at least a glimpse of Andrew. She could picture how he would look, so proud of what she'd done.

He loved her. The thought had woken her every morning and it had been the last thing on her mind before she slept each night. Etiquette dictated they remain apart come the night but she had not yet had to sleep in the hall with the majority of the castle residents. Instead, she'd been given a room at the top of the tower, eventually to become a guard room when the keep was finished but a place of her own until she went home.

The voice of the bishop faded away as she thought about going back. She had tried not to think about it, easy to do as she dedicated her every waking hour to getting the chapel done in time. Now it was done, the thoughts were creeping back in. She would have to go home to find her mother and look after her.

She wanted to stay but she couldn't. She wanted nothing more than to lay in Andrew's bed with him and feel those strong arms of his wrap around her, keep her safe from the perils of this time. After he rescued her in the wood, she felt as if nothing bad could ever happen again as long as he was around.

Something brought her out of her thoughts. A noise in front of her. Above the sound of the bishop she heard it again. A creaking groaning sound. It faded away to nothing.

The people inside the chapel hadn't moved but she had a worrying feeling that the sound was that of stones shifting, pulling the wooden falsework with it. At least the falsework would stop any damage from occurring but once the service was over she would need to get the ladders out and examine where that noise was coming from.

"We bless this chapel and I bless personally the master mason. Where is Beth Dagless?"

"She's here," a voice said in front of Beth. People turned and looked at her, squeezing aside as best they could to let her walk into the chapel. She had to force her way forward and she was more than halfway through to the altar when she happened to glance up. She looked down, her stomach suddenly lurching as she glanced up for a second time. She hadn't been imagining it.

The falsework was gone. The arches were not being supported. It was the stonework that had groaned and it was groaning because the mortar hadn't set. How long had the falsework been gone? Who removed it? She froze in place, the bishop calling her over from a long way away.

"We have to get out," she said at once.

It was like a bad dream. Everyone just looked at her but no one moved. Did they think she was joking?

"We have to get out, now!" she shouted, waving toward the door.

"Come and be blessed, my child," the bishop said behind her. "God praises you for your glorious work on His chapel."

She scanned the crowd quickly as the ceiling above her groaned again. A quick look up and she saw the cracks spreading, the keystone right above her head had shifted two inches downward. Any further and it would come out, taking the rest of the ceiling with it.

Andrew suddenly appeared next to her. "What is it?" he asked. "Why do you look so worried?"

"The ceiling," she said, pointing upward. "It's coming down. You have to get them all out of here right now."

He looked where she was pointing as the people continued to stare without moving. There was a louder noise and a few of the crowd looked up, spotting the stones starting to shift and shake, dust beginning to fall from them.

"Dinnae shout," Andrew said to her. "They'll panic and be crushed in the doorway. "This way."

He grabbed hold of her and pulled her through the crowd toward the open door. As they went he spoke low to the people nearest to him. They began talking to others and a ripple spread through the crowd.

Beth was incredulous. Somehow his method was working. The whispers reached the doorway and the path was cleared, those who had crammed into the entrance and overflowed it were moving away, beckoning to the rest.

As Beth reached the door she heard a creaking sound louder than any before. The keystone nearest the altar suddenly fell free. After that everything seemed to happen at once.

The springers crumbled with the keystone, falling through the air and landing with an enormous crash. "This way," Andrew shouted, darting back into the chapel and grabbing hold of people as panic broke out, shoving them out the door. His men were doing the same as more of the ceiling began to collapse around them.

Beth couldn't believe what was happening. One minute she was listening to the bishop praise her work and the next the chapel ceiling was collapsing in front of her eyes. She waved people away further from the chapel, worried the whole thing would crumble.

She caught sight of Andrew in the middle of it all, stones falling around him. One hit his shoulder. He fell and she gasped but then he was up once more, continuing to guide people out.

She lost sight of him again as a mass of screaming bodies ran past her. There was an ear splitting sound as the last of the ceiling fell in an enormous thud. A plume of dust rose up but all Beth could hear was the ringing in her ears.

Were there still people screaming? She walked forward toward the church, seeing white ghosts emerging, coughing, blood falling from head wounds. "Andrew!" she shouted but even if he answered her ears were ringing too loudly for her to hear it.

Further in she spotted the bishop laid on his front, a stone on top of his back.

She shoved it off him, trying and failing to drag his still form across the rubble strewn floor. A hand appeared next to her, taking hold of the bishop by the shoulders.

She looked. It was Andrew. Blood was flowing freely down his cheek as he pulled the bishop from the chapel.

"I'm so sorry," Beth muttered as they reached the courtyard. "It's all my fault."

Andrew didn't answer. He was already back inside the chapel, helping his men to move stone, reaching down to free the people still trapped. Beth ran to help.

The next few minutes were a blur of shifting stone and helping one person after another. Only when Andrew was certain that no one was left under the rubble did he finally emerge, sitting on the rushes outside and wiping the blood from his eyes.

Duff MacLeish emerged from the crowd to stand in front of him, arms folded. "If that was a plot to kill me, it didnae work, did it?"

Andrew got to his feet, sounding more tired than angry. "If I was plotting to kill you, do you think I'd be in there at the same time?"

"I'm thinking maybe you got the timing wrong. The bishop wanted to speak to me after the service. Is he in your thrall or was the plan to kill us both?"

"Och, dinnae talk daft."

"You invite me to the blessing and then the roof collapses. I'm supposed to think what? That it's a coincidence? I was not born yesterday, laddie."

"It was her fault," someone shouted, pointing at Beth. "She said it was finished."

"Aye, she did," another voice added.

Beth felt all eyes on her. Even Duff turned to glare. "Well, lassie? What do you have to say for yourself?"

Chapter Seventeen

As Andrew prepared to defend Beth, a plume of dust drifted out from the chapel, falling on the dead and wounded. The injured were being tended to by James but it was obvious some of them would never awaken. Would the bishop? Was there a curse on the MacIntyres? Was God himself trying to kill Andrew?

As he'd dragged the last of the victims out from under the fallen stone, he thought of Fenella. She had told him he should look up sometime. Was this what she was referring to? Should he have noticed the ceiling was about to collapse?

"Perhaps your master mason is not as good as she claims," Duff said, taking a step toward Beth. "People are dead and dying lassie. Have you nothing to say for yourself?"

Andrew marched over, separating the two of them. "You will calm yourself MacLeish."

"Calm myself? I was almost killed."

"As were many of my people."

Beth looked up at them both, her face pale. "The falsework," she said. "It was the falsework."

"What are you talking about?" Duff asked.

"The falsework. It was holding up the arches until the mortar set." She was talking more to herself than to either of them. "It shouldn't have been taken down yet. Someone must have removed it."

"Explain yourself," Duff said. "Before I take you into my custody."

"You'll do nothing of the sort," Andrew said, his voice cold.

"Are you going to stop me?"

"I will do what it takes to protect her."

"So you want a war over a woman do you?"

Beth stepped between them, turning to face Duff. "The falsework was holding up the stone until the mortar set. I said it was to stay up, that it wasn't ready to come down yet but someone took it out. They must have known what would happen."

"A likely story. You're just trying to cover up your incompetence."

"I'm telling you someone took it down."

"And who would do that?"

A voice spoke from their left. "I know."

The three of them looked that way. One of the kitchen girls was holding up her hand. "I was on my way to feed the chickens just before the bishop arrived."

"And?" Duff snapped. "What did you see?"

"I saw Derek coming out of the church carrying the falsework."

"Och, you're a wee servant. How do you even know what falsework looks like?"

The girl stood taller, glancing from Duff to Beth, a shy smile on her face. "I've been watching her. I want to be a master mason when I grow up."

"A kitchen girl becoming a master mason? Now I've heard everything."

Beth smiled at the girl. "Are you sure you saw him?"

"He took it behind the chapel and then he came back out without it. I didnae know the mortar hadnae set. I thought Beth had told him to do it."

"Well there's one way to settle this," Andrew said, setting off through the crowd of people. "Let's go look."

They walked behind the chapel together. Andrew kicked at the piled up rushes by the nave wall, revealing the falsework underneath.

"Where is my son?" Duff roared, spinning around on the spot. "Derek!"

"He took Beth out to look at the battlements," Andrew said. "Just before the service began."

Of course, he thought. Derek didn't want her to see what he'd done. He knew if she went inside she'd spot the missing falsework at once. "Where is he?"

"Here," a voice said from the portcullis. Andrew looked over to see Gillis holding Derek by the scruff of the neck. "Caught him trying to run off. I wondered why he was sprinting like the hounds of hell were after him. What's happened here?"

"Why dinnae you speak up and tell us all?" Duff asked. "What have you done, laddie?"

"I did it for you, father."

"What?" Duff roared. "Are you saying it's true. You brought down that ceiling? You almost killed me? Why would you do such a thing?"

"I didnae know you were going to be here. If you'd told me you were coming, I could have warned you."

"I am Duff MacLeish, laird of my clan. I do not need to tell you anything. Why did you do it? Your answer better be good."

"I thought if Andrew was dead there'd be no reason for me to stay here. I could come home and we could rule the highlands together as father and son."

"You set the mercenaries on him at the loch, didn't you?"

A slow nod.

"Did you burn Pluscarden too?"

Another nod. "My man Rufus but I was paying him."

Duff turned away in disgust, looking at Andrew with his hand outstretched. "I owe you an apology. I sent a snake into your midst without even knowing it. Will you shake my hand?"

Andrew took it, feeling the eyes of everyone on him.

"You can execute him yourself or I'll take him back and deal with him for this atrocity. Name whatever you wish and it shall be done."

Andrew looked at Beth, seeing the sparkle in her eyes. He knew at once what to do. "What your son did, he did for the right reasons. He wanted the clans united as do I. If you would grant me one wish it is that we put aside our feuds and come together to fend off the English."

"Done."

"Please forgive me, father," Derek wailed, tears running down his cheeks. "I'm sorry."

"Save your blather for the executioner. You have burned, you have killed, you have destroyed. Tears will not save you."

There was a groan from the ground and the bishop sat up slowly, shaking his head. "I have a suggestion," he said, getting to his feet. "If you would hear it, MacLeish. You have founded an abbey at Melrose, have you not?"

"Aye," Duff replied.

"Derek, do you wish to repent of your sins?"

"I do," Derek shouted from the portcullis, throwing himself onto his knees, his hands clasped together in the air. "Forgive me, I beg you. I don't want to go to hell."

The bishop nodded before turning back to Duff. "Let him be the first novice to enter the monastery grounds. There your son will learn the true meaning of repentance and humility."

"Will you accept that?" Duff asked Andrew. "I leave the decision up to you for it is you who has been most aggrieved by his actions."

Andrew turned to Beth, seeing the slightest nod of her head. "I agree," he said.

"Oh, thank you," Derek called out, crawling through the mud on his knees. "You are kind and just, my laird."

"Get up out of the mud," Duff said. "And stand over there until I am ready to leave. Say not another word or the monastery may have a novice entering with no tongue to sing their blessed psalms."

He turned his back on his son, facing Andrew and Beth as they stood together. "I will take him back to my castle and to the monastery thereafter. I will send a dozen of my laborers here as a gesture toward your forgiveness. Use them to help rebuild your chapel."

"I thank you for your generosity," Andrew replied. "Now I must tend to the wounded."

"Of course. We will talk of our union soon. I have a daughter coming of age that I would have you marry. That will cement the bonds between us."

Andrew shook his head. "That will not be possible but Gillis is next in line to the lairdship. Perhaps you might introduce him to your lassie."

Duff nodded, his eyes narrowing as he looked at Beth. "I think I understand. You have given your heart to another. In the usual course of events I would mock such sentimentality in a laird but these are not usual times. The union of our clans will hold despite your rejection of my offer. Farewell, MacIntyre. Until we meet again."

He walked away, grabbing hold of Derek as he went and shoving him over to their waiting horses. Andrew turned to Beth. "You said you would stay until the chapel was complete. Will you keep that oath?"

"I will," she nodded. "Now go help them. We can talk later."

He left her in conversation with the bishop as he began moving through the crowd. James had already taken charge of the walking wounded. They had gathered by the infirmary. Other MacIntyres were tending to the more seriously injured.

He gathered his men to him. "Bring me stretchers of canvas and get as many as you can into the infirmary. We will have need of much water from the well and as many cloths as you can find."

"Aye," they said as one, moving away and getting to work at once. Andrew looked around him. Beth was still talking to the bishop. He caught a snippet of their conversation, her explaining the advantages of stone vaulting over wood and the reasons why falsework was so important.

Duff and Derek had ridden away. He found himself thinking about everything that had happened since the fire at Pluscarden. Should he have spotted that Derek was responsible? Would his father have known? He shook his head. It was not the time for introspection. That could take place once the wounded were tended to.

As he headed over to the infirmary to assist, he couldn't help feeling a great joy. He knew it was selfish in the midst of so much destruction but it was there nonetheless. She had said she would stay until the chapel was completed. He had dreaded the end of the service for he knew that was when she planned to bid him farewell and return to her own time.

The collapse of the vault was awful but it also meant a stay of execution. He could snatch a precious few more weeks with her. It would never be enough. He wanted a lifetime but he could not have it. She had insisted on returning to her mother no matter how much he pleaded that she might change her mind.

If he could not have a lifetime with her, a few weeks would have to do. He would just have to make the most of the time they had left and then survive on the memories afterward.

Chapter Eighteen

It was long after dark when Beth finally stopped work for the night. As the sun had set, she had lit candles around the chapel, allowing her enough light to continue removing the fallen stone with the help of the laborers.

"How bad is it?" Rory asked.

"Not as bad as I first thought. "We can reuse many of these stones. I think perhaps a guard this time though to ensure the falsework is not interfered with."

"I doubt that will happen again now Derek is gone."

"Nevertheless just to be sure."

An hour later the wind began to grow. One by one the candles were snuffed out and eventually relighting them became pointless. Beth called a halt until dawn the next day.

She watched the laborers heading out of the castle to their villages. They all looked exhausted. She was not surprised. Her limbs ached as she made her way to the castle keep.

She had missed dinner, not wanting to waste any time in shoring up what was left of the roof. A few of the slate tiles had fallen but most had remained in place on the timber framework. It was only the vaulting itself that had collapsed.

She made a rough calculation of how long it would take to repair. They might have a working chapel in a month though the plastering would have to wait until the following year. The important thing was getting enough lime mortar and she would need to ask Andrew if he could afford it alongside all his other expenses.

She had already increased his building costs many times over with the work she had set in place. She was starting to realize that the job of master mason wasn't just about the work, it required some financial acumen and tact as well in explaining why costs kept going up.

She entered the keep, closing the door behind her to keep the draft out and the heat in. The fire would have died down in the great hall but the warmth remained in the stones for many hours afterwards, heating the corridors and staircases until late into the night as long as doors were opened as little as possible.

She passed the hall, hearing the sound of snoring coming from within. Up the flight of stairs she went, heading for her room. She opened the door and walked into it, surprised to find Andrew sitting on the chair by the window, looking out into the courtyard.

"You frightened the life out of me," she said as she closed the door behind her. "I thought etiquette meant you couldn't be alone in the same room as an unmarried woman at night."

"I care not for etiquette this evening," he replied. "I thought I was going to lose you today."

"In the collapse, you mean? You made sure I was safely out."

"Nay, I mean I thought you were going back to your own time."

"Oh."

She crossed the room to the ewer of water, splashing a handful onto her face, wiping away the dust and grime of her work.

"What's she like?" Beth asked as she turned back to face Andrew. "Duff's daughter?"

"She will be happy enough with Gillis. I have seen them courting before now though I would never tell Duff that."

"Is that your only reason for turning down his proposal?"

"There is another reason."

"Which is?"

"We should not talk of that."

She frowned. "Why not?"

"Because you wish to return to your own time and it would only complicate things for us both to discuss it now."

"You came to my bedchamber. What did you want to discuss? The weather?"

"I wanted to discuss marrying you."

Beth almost fell over. "What? You know I can't."

"Why not? I love you. You love me. You have done so much for me and my people. You have begun a castle that will last for generations. Why not stay and see the work done?"

"Because I have to go home." She saw how hurt he looked. "I don't want to go but I have to find my mom. She needs taking care of. She's...she's ill."

"You didnae say."

"She's dying, all right? She hasn't got a lot of time left and I can't leave her on her own. I'm all she's got in the world. Oh, why am I even trying to explain? You wouldn't understand."

"I nursed my own mother through her illness. I watched her die slowly and painfully. Dinnae tell me I wouldn't understand."

"Then you understand why I must go."

His eyes flamed. "Aye, of course I do. That disnae make it any easier to take. I love you, Beth. I want you to stay."

"And I can't. I'm sorry, I truly am."

"I know that." He looked aggrieved but the look softened as he stood up. "I know that," he said again, his voice quieter.

"I'm sorry," she said, crossing the floor to him. "I wish I could stay. Truly I do. I want for nothing more than to marry you and make this castle my home but I must go back to my mom."

He nodded slowly, his hands slipping into hers. "Then you should go to her."

"I will miss you. More than anything in the world, I will miss you."

"I will miss you too." He leaned forward, brushing a lock of hair away from her face. "More than you could possibly know."

His hand slid around the back of her neck, drawing her toward him. He dipped his head and then they were kissing.

Beth felt a surge of heat coursing through her body as they embraced.

He pushed her back until she was crushed against the tapestry behind her. He continued to kiss her, his arms holding her in place, as if he never wanted to let go.

She felt the heat inside her grow as his hands moved down her back and then up once more, sliding over the shoulders of her dress, easing them down.

She went to move away but any resistance inside her melted when he began to kiss her neck, his rough lips bringing a gasp out of her.

The dress fell from her. How had that even happened? The kirtle was gone a moment later and then she was naked, the tapestry digging into her back as he ran his hands over her body.

There was a gust of wind and the candles blew out leaving only the slight glow of the fire in the hearth.

Beth looked at him in the half-light as he stood back from her. She watched him pull down his hose to reveal...

She couldn't look down there. If she did that, she would melt into a puddle on the floor. The air was so filled with tension it seemed to hum.

Once he was naked he crossed back to her, lifting her straight into his arms and carrying her over to the bed.

He lay her down gently on her back. He remained standing in the glow of the fire, hunger in his eyes. "I love you," he said quietly. "And tonight you will not sleep alone."

"I love you too," she replied as he climbed onto her.

She said nothing else. His lips were on hers and for a long time she said nothing at all.

With her eyes closed her other senses were heightened. She could feel everything, every scar and taut muscle on his body, even the thud of his heart through his chest.

She remembered that night for the rest of her life, the fire dying down to smoldering embers as the two of them lay together under the blankets, the highlander holding her close, as if he never wanted to let her go.

Outside the wind died down, the clouds clearing as the stars came out one by one. They twinkled high above the castle while down in the tower, she was held by the highlander, praying the night would last forever, wishing that morning would never come.

Her wishes were not answered. The sun rose on their sleeping forms all too soon and then it was time for them to part once more.

Chapter Nineteen

It was a journey Andrew did not want to make. So many times in his life he had traveled from the old hall to the new castle to observe the progress of the building work. When he was little it had been on foot but once he was old enough to ride he had more often than not gone on horseback beside his father's noble steed.

While he was being shown the work, his father would look down at him and say, "One day, lad, all this will be yours."

Andrew would nod and smile but he had no real understanding of what that meant. He knew now. It did not mean just the stones, it meant the people working there, the lands both inside and outside the castle grounds.

It had become his all too soon and after the death of his parents, he had traveled alone between the castle and the old hall, considering both his home.

He recalled the journeys alone, the road seeming very desolate once he became laird. He felt immense sorrow at the loss he had suffered but that pain was nothing to that he endured as he rode with Beth sitting in front of him on the day she was to return home.

It was only a short distance from the castle to Pluscarden, less than a day's ride. He wished it was miles and miles, the journey was almost over and yet it had barely begun.

When they got there she would be leaving forever. He had tried many times to come to terms with that fact but it still cut him deep every time he looked at her, knowing how he would soon never see that smiling face again, those sparkling eyes, that mind of hers, so much sharper than any he'd ever known.

She was going home.

It was a pain that stabbed at him over and over as they rode like walking barefoot with a thorn in his heel. He could not ignore it no matter how hard he tried.

The chapel was finished and she was going home. The snow had begun to fall an hour earlier, coating the fields with white like an enormous blanket dropped from the skies. Winter was here and there would be no more building work until spring.

It was as if the heavens had waited until she was done to send winter along to take over the highlands. The chapel was complete. The bishop had returned and blessed the highlands, the castle, and her.

The falsework remained in place. It would not come down until she was long gone. "I will see it in my time," she had said that very morning as they prepared for the ride. "Hopefully it will still be standing."

Andrew had barely grunted in response. She looked hurt by his silence and on the ride she had said not a word. He dared not speak to her. He needed to get used to the idea of life without her. Engaging her in conversation would not help that.

It had been a perfect month in many ways though with a black cloud looming over him for every moment of it. That night they had spent together had not been repeated.

He had only to close his eyes and he was back in the bed with her, nothing but the two of them in the darkness. It was the most perfect night of his life and that was why he had not returned to her chamber for the rest of her stay. It would make letting her go impossible.

He knew why she had to leave. Knowing her reasons only made him love her all the more. She was willing to put her own desires to one side to tend for another, that was the depth of her compassion. He could only admire that.

They reached Pluscarden just after noon. The cellarium had been completed, the windows in the correct place. The stairs to the floors above were wooden, easy to chop away if there was an attack, not that Andrew was expecting one.

Since the alliance between the MacIntyres and the MacLeishes had been announced the other clans of the highlands had come together to negotiate terms. Soon, if things went well, the highlands would be united and then the Normans would have something to fear. They could bring their entire army north of the border but they would find only death waiting for them with a united Scotland.

He had spoken to Fenella only once since the collapse of the chapel roof. In her chair she had leaned back, the cat on her lap, nodding as he told her all that had happened.

"Perhaps she came back to unite the clans," she said when he was done. "And now that task is done, she is supposed to leave."

"Is there no potion that could make her stay? No spell you could cast to persuade her to be my bride?"

"Even if there were, you would not want to use them, would you?"

He sighed. "I suppose not. Do you have any advice at all?"

"Aye, I do as it happens. Do you remember what I told you last time you were here?"

"To look up, not that I listened in time."

"This time I tell you only that you should look down."

"Look down? When?"

"When the moment is right you'll know."

She would not be drawn on any more detail and so Andrew was left with only a hint of what he might do to make her stay. Given that weeks had passed and gluing his eyes to the ground had revealed nothing, he suspected whatever he was supposed to see, he had missed it.

Outside the hall, he clambered off his horse, helping Beth down to the ground. "This is it," she said.

"Aye," he replied, saying no more.

The building site was empty. Andrew had told all the workers they would be paid for the day but they were to stay away. He was still working out how he was going to pay to get all the work done.

There was not enough spare money to go around. Even the work on Pluscarden abbey had slowed to almost nothing. At this rate, his hall might be built by next winter but the abbey would take until the day of reckoning itself.

Beth walked over to the pit where the cellarium had been built. A rough wooden bridge had been built over it to the door at ground level. "Will it happen here, do you think?" she asked, turning to face him. "Or the bedroom itself?"

"I dinnae know," he said, hoping it wouldn't happen at all, wishing once again that she would stay with him. He would never see that beautiful face again, those eyes that shimmered like sparkling dawn light on a crystal clear loch.

"I will never forget you," she said, holding out a hand to him.

He didn't take it. He couldn't. He might not be able to let go again.

"Goodbye then," she said.

"Farewell, lass. I thank you for all you've done."

"Look after this place, won't you?"

"I will that."

She leaned forward and kissed his cheek, a tear rolling from her eye as she turned away and walked through the doorway.

Nothing happened.

She spun around, looking back at him. "I'm still here."

"Aye," he said, hope rising in him. "So you are."

"It must be the bedroom door after all."

She walked into the hall, along the low stones that marked the corridor. It was beaten earth and covered in snow but when finished it would be tiled or flagged depending on what he could afford.

He followed her, stopping by the one remaining part of the original building. The doorway into the bedroom where he was born.

"This is it," she said, looking at him and starting to cry.

He couldn't look at her any longer. She was going and he would never see her again. He looked down at her feet, frowning as he spotted something. It had been hidden under the snow until she walked by, her foot revealing something that sparkled in the light.

"What's that you're looking at?" she asked, looking down where his eyes were fixed. She gasped, leaning down and grabbing the object from the floor.

"What is it?" he asked. "What have you found?"

She held her hand out for him to see. It was a silver locket on a long thin chain. "This was my mother's," she said, opening it to reveal an image of a baby so real, Andrew was shocked.

"Who can paint so well?"

"It's not a painting. It's a photo of me." Her fingers curled around the locket. "Do you know what this means? It means she's here. She must have come through time after all."

"If she is here," Andrew said, wrapping his hand around hers. "We will find her."

Chapter Twenty

The hall was a hive of activity. The tables that were usually pushed to the side of the room except during meals had been left in place for days, covered in letters coming and going, maps and charts filling the remaining space. There had not been a single moment when people were not entering or leaving the castle on the most urgent business.

Beth sat at the top table, realizing she was doing exactly what her mother used to do. She had the locket around her neck and was squeezing it so tightly in her hand her fingers had turned white.

Scouts had been sent in every possible direction to look for Janet. Each day reports came back but none of them positive. It was as if she'd vanished off the face of the earth.

Each morning Beth awoke with a new found hope but as the day wore on, she would become more anxious, feeling a dread rise up in her that the report when it came would tell her they'd been too late.

She hated the thought of her mother dying somewhere far from her, not knowing where her daughter was.

It had been a week since she'd been to the old hall. In the time that had passed she had waited anxiously for news. Andrew had taken charge of the search, gathering men to him from the moment they returned to the castle, telling them to drop everything and start looking.

Duff MacLeish had sent a dozen of his own men when he'd heard. Boats had been sent to the islands, monks had taken messages to monasteries in England. All she could do was wait and it was killing her.

Another messenger came in, running straight up to Andrew and Beth. "Yes?" Andrew said, looking up from his maps.

It was Gillis looking back at him. "You have news?"

"I think you should come down to the infirmary," Gillis said, his face pale. "At once."

Beth was already running, darting between people and out, reaching the bottom of the stairs in moments. She looked about her, seeing only the faces of the castle inhabitants she had come to know so well.

James had his back to her, helping someone into the infirmary. Whoever was with him was wearing a huge winter cloak, the snow settling on their shoulders and turning them white.

"Mom?" Beth shouted, sprinting across the courtyard. The figure with James turned around and then Beth began to cry. "Mom! It's you."

Her mother looked back at her, a smile breaking out across her face. "Beth."

Beth threw her arms around her mother, holding her tight to her for a very long time as both of them began to cry.

Eventually James separated them. "She is exhausted," he said. "We should get her into the infirmary."

"I'm all right," Janet replied, staggering slightly as she spoke. "I'm just not used to horse riding."

"Come on," James said, taking her arm and leading her into the infirmary. "Let's get you sat down at least."

Beth followed closely behind, watching nervously as her mother was helped into the nearest bed. She looked pale and drawn, her eyes still filled with tears.

"Where have you been?" Beth asked. "What happened?"

"Not now," James said. "She must rest. Here, Janet. Drink this."

He held a horn cup to her lips and she sipped the thick green liquid within before falling back on the bolster, her eyes closing.

"We should give her some time," Andrew said, appearing next to her. "She is exhausted. Come, we'll wait outside."

"I'm not going anywhere," she replied, kneeling next to the bed. "I'm staying right here."

The next few hours were the tensest she'd ever known. Andrew stood silently beside her the entire time, saying nothing.

James brought a damp cloth for Janet's forehead, replacing it now and then.

Sitting beside the bed, Beth looked at the face of her mother. She felt a huge relief that she was still alive and yet mingled with that relief was fear that Janet would not again wake up, that she would never know what had happened to her during the time they'd been apart.

The bells had been rung for dinner before Janet opened her eyes again, turning to look at Beth as she did so, a smile once again spreading across her face. "I feared I had dreamed that I was here," she said, running a hand across her daughter's cheek. "Is it really you?"

"Yes, mom. It's me. What happened to you?"

"I will tell you all about that later. First I want to know what happened to you. It looks as if you've been here all your life. I hardly recognized you."

Beth told her everything. From stepping through the doorway to seeing the hall burn down. She glossed over being accused of starting the fire, moving onto finding her way to the castle.

She talked about the building work, fixing the battlement walls, rebuilding the chapel, not mentioning the collapse for fear of upsetting her. "And who is this?" Janet asked, sitting up slowly in the bed, examining Andrew from behind a furrowed brow.

"This is Andrew, laird of the MacIntyres."

Andrew nodded. "A pleasure to meet you at last. You've given my men some trouble tracking you down."

"Here," Beth said, holding out the locket. "Take it back."

"You found it?" Janet said, sitting bolt upright. "I thought I'd lost that forever." She shook her head. "You should keep it. It was going to be yours anyway once..." Her voice faded away then she smiled again. "Not that it matters. I can't tell you how much better I've felt since coming back here. I swear I might live to be a hundred."

She swung her legs out of the bed, getting slowly to her feet. She stood in front of Andrew, looking him up and down. "Well, well. Andrew MacIntyre. I always dreamed about meeting you and now it finally happens. I hope you've been good to my daughter."

"Mom!" Beth said. "Don't talk to him like that."

"I see the look in his eyes. I've been around long enough to know what that look means."

"And what does it mean?" Andrew asked, looking amused by her anger.

"It means you better propose to her before this goes any further. I wondered which Dagless you were going to marry and now I know. I never would have guessed it would be my daughter, not in a million years."

"As a matter of fact I have proposed," Andrew said, smiling. "Though she said no."

"And what did you go and do a stupid thing like that for?" Janet asked, turning her attention to Beth.

"I couldn't marry him. I needed to find you."

"That's the stupidest thing I ever heard. You have the chance for happiness with a man who clearly worships you and you turn him down to babysit your own mother. You turn around right now and agree to marry him. Go on."

"Mom!"

James could hide his laughter no longer, he walked rapidly away, his hand covering his mouth.

Beth blushed wildly. "Sorry about her."

"She's right," Andrew replied. "You should marry me."

"Is that what you call a proposal?" Janet asked. "You're not too old to be spanked yourself Mr MacIntyre so you just ask her properly before I drop dead of old age."

The sound of James's continuing laughter echoed from the far end of the infirmary.

Andrew turned to Beth, sinking to one knee, his hand held up to hers. "Will you marry me?"

"Of course I will," she replied, jumping into his arms and almost knocking him over.

"There," Janet said, rubbing her hands together. "That's settled. Now where can I get something to eat? I'm absolutely starving."

Beth turned to look at her. "You still need to tell us what happened to you."

"Plenty of time for that later. First we need to start planning a wedding. Tell me you have a decent kitchen for me to make the cake."

She walked out of the infirmary into the courtyard, beckoning for them to follow.

"Are you glad you found her?" James asked over Beth's shoulder, still chuckling to himself. "She seems quite the woman."

"That's mom," she replied, shaking her head. "We better go after her before she starts redecorating the entire place for you." She looked up at Andrew. "What? Why are you looking at me like that?"

"Because I thought I had lost you forever and instead you just agreed to marry me. Am I not allowed to look at you?"

"Come on you two lovebirds," Janet called back to them. "Lots to do."

"Coming," they said in unison, heading out of the infirmary and following her across the courtyard.

Andrew's hand slipped into Beth's as they walked. She looked down at it briefly. It felt exactly right, as if that was what she'd always been missing without even knowing it, the hold of the highlander.

Chapter Twenty-One

The baldric had been specially made for the occasion. Andrew looked down at it and was once again struck by the vibrancy of the colors.

His boots weren't spotless but it was still winter after all. The mud had frozen under the snow but each day it was churned up afresh by the residents of the castle coming and going across the courtyard, making preparations for the wedding.

Andrew stood outside the chapel, Gillis beside him. "Are you ready for this?" Gillis asked.

"It'll be your turn next," Andrew replied.

Gillis slapped him on the back. "Then I will look as nervous as you."

"Och, I'm not nervous man."

"Then why do you look so pale?"

"Quit your blathering at me. I'm in no mood for it."

"Then you better get inside. They're all waiting."

He headed through the doorway. The chapel was crammed with people. He couldn't help comparing it to last time it had been this full. On that day the ceiling had collapsed and several people had died. He glanced up at the falsework, as if afraid it might have been removed once again.

It was all safe. The abbot of Melrose was standing at the front of the chapel. Next to him was the bishop. The two of them nodded as Andrew walked toward them. He stopped when he reached them.

"Good to see you again Andrew," the bishop said. "Are you well?"

"Quite well, your Grace," he replied. "And Walter. I am glad you could come."

"I would not have missed it," the abbot replied. "Nor would she, I'm sure." He nodded toward the back of the church as the crowd fell silent.

Andrew turned in time to see Beth appear. She was holding a bouquet of flowers. How had they even found them in the depths of winter? Her dress was whiter than the snow outside and her face hidden behind a veil as she made her way slowly down the aisle, the people smiling as she passed them by.

Her mother stood next to her, looking far better than on the day she'd returned to them. She still hadn't explained what happened to her while they were apart, insisting that they focus instead on the wedding preparations. "All in good time," was all she would say when they asked.

Andrew was beginning to think she would never tell them. Not that it mattered. What mattered was standing facing him as the abbot began to speak to the crowd. "Under the sight of God we come together today to bless the union of Beth Dagless and Andrew MacIntyre. I stand before you as a humble servant of God and ask you all to pray for them and for all of us."

The crowd murmured an amen. The bishop took over. "We all of us here and across the world have the power within us for both forgiveness and vengeance. I was grievously injured when the ceiling of this very chapel collapsed. Many died that day and vengeance was talked about in hushed voices that I could not help but overhear."

He paused, allowing a smile to spread across his face. "Anger would tear apart the clans of the highlands. Compassion would bring them together. The MacLeishes are here today as are the MacIntyres. That is the power of forgiveness and it is a force far mightier than the sinful that would attempt to tear our people asunder. Andrew MacIntyre is a good man and I do not say that lightly. If he wishes to marry this woman I give them both my eternal blessing. Amen."

The abbot nodded, stepping forward as the bishop retreated. "A great building such as this glories God and brings His light to shine upon those of his subjects who worship Him with pure heart and spirit. A great union is a stronger sign still that love is in our hearts and God in the souls of all those present here today."

"Och, will you not get on with it?" Duff MacLeish shouted from the back of the church. "We're freezing our arses off back here."

Andrew tried not to laugh as the abbot turned pink, losing the thread of what he was saying.

"The vows," Andrew whispered.

"Oh yes. Would you, Andrew MacIntyre, take this woman to be your wife from this day until the end of your life, to hold and keep in safety and love, to worship and honor with your obedient spirit and all the blood of the clan that is in your body."

"Aye," Andrew replied, not taking his eyes from Beth.

"And would you, Beth Dagless, take this man to be your husband from this day until the end of your life, to hold and worship, to obey and honor with your spirit, your soul, and your heart?"

"Aye." There was just a hint of a Scottish accent to her voice.

"Then I declare these two husband and wife and to you all I ask you to give good cheer to Laird and Lady MacIntyre."

A resounding shout went up around the chapel as Beth lifted her veil, revealing those sparkling eyes that he swore grew brighter with every passing day.

"You may kiss," the abbot said over the noise.

Andrew leaned toward his bride, embracing her firmly as the noise around him died away. All he felt was her and nothing else. Nothing else would ever matter as much as she did.

"Now onto the hall before we starve," Duff shouted above the cheers. "I hear yon lass has prepared a feast."

"If by yon lass," Janet said, "you mean me, you better address me more politely." She glared at him as Beth rolled her eyes at Andrew.

"They seem to hate each other," he said. "This should be fun."

"I'm sure it will," Beth replied with a twinkle in her eyes. "Though I get the feeling they might end up sitting together by the end of the day.

The feast went on for many hours. The bishop making the first speech when the time came.

"I want to say a few words," he said, waving his arms to silence the revelers. "As a token of the church's thanks for the glorious chapel you have built here, and for the abbey you have founded, Andrew, I have been authorized by the council of the north to give you the rights to the quarry by the water."

Andrew was speechless. In one fell swoop his financial problems were over. The quarry by the water was one of the richest quarries in all the highlands. He could not only finish rebuilding the castle at almost no cost, he would be able sell the extra stone to finance all the other work.

"It's not a free gift," Gillis whispered in his ear. "He knows that way you'll get Pluscarden abbey built faster."

"Aye," Andrew whispered back. "But what's the harm in that?"

Duff stood up next. "I consider Andrew MacIntyre the reason my son is alive, not dead and the reason I am enjoying this delicious meal. I thank you too bishop whatever your name is. This man today has lived up to the name of MacIntyre and I am proud to be in a union with him. May we bring hell itself down onto the English's sorry arses. Sorry, bishop."

The bishop nodded benevolently before tucking back into his chicken leg.

The abbot stood up. "I want you all to know that I love this man and this woman who have married here today. Even the noisy oaf at the back has my love.

Duff, you'll be pleased to know that Derek is settling in well at Melrose. He confessed his sins and repents them all in fear of the everlasting fires of hell that come to all sinners. He is the perfect novice and perhaps one day you will forgive him his sins as God has.

"Perhaps," Duff shouted back. "We'll see. Now enough with the bloody speeches. Let's get back to eating."

A cheer went up. Andrew looked at Beth and smiled. It had finally happened. For so long he thought he would lose her and now she was his wife. He could not have been happier.

Beth's prediction came true. By the time she tiptoed out with Andrew her mother was sitting almost on the lap of Duff MacLeish, feeding him one morsel after another.

"How does it feel to be married?" Andrew asked, slipping his hand into hers as they made their way up to his bed chamber.

"I've had worse days," she replied with a grin.

He pushed open the door, stepping aside to let her enter. Once they were both in, he locked the door, and then poked the fire to bring it back to life.

"Are you glad you stayed here?" he asked. "Don't miss anything about your own time?"

She shook her head. "Not a thing. Where else would I get to help build a whole new castle?"

"The bishop thinks you were sent by God."

"What do you think?"

"I think I'm glad we're alone at last and I'm glad you decided to stay."

"I had to stay. You need me to help you build a castle strong enough to defend against English invasion. Don't you mind though?"

"Mind what?"

"That I'm English."

"Perhaps I'll let just one English invade my castle."

"Is that a promise?"

He took hold of her, lifting her onto the bed. In the great hall the feast continued with laughter and song. In the laird's bed chamber the fire died down as the laird and his new bride lay together in the darkness.

Outside the snow continued to fall, carpeting the entire castle and all the surrounding land in a white blanket. By the morning it would be a foot deep. Neither Andrew nor Beth would notice a thing. They were far too busy making up for lost time.

Epilogue

Derek was praying in the chapel when they came in. He was on his knees, head bowed before the altar. Whispering quietly, he had just glanced up at the cross, thanking the Lord for this second chance at life. Then the door opened and the strangers began talking.

He was back at the chapel where his whole life had changed. The abbot had come to him a week earlier and told him to make the pilgrimage back to MacIntyre castle.

He didn't want to go back. In the year since he'd been sworn in as a novice he'd grown used to the monastic life. It had a simplicity and purity to it that he respected. He heard little about life back at the castle. When news reached the abbey of the birth of Andrew and Beth's child, he rejoiced silently, praising God for His mercy and His wisdom. During his sleep he was plagued by dreams of what he'd done in the past, glad when they rose for matins each night. He would walk with the others into the small wooden abbey church, unable to shake the guilt until the singing began. Only then could he rejoice in this second chance he'd been given to prove his repentance and to pray for all those he'd hurt in the past.

He never expected to leave the abbey again but he could no more disobey the order of the abbot than he could float over the mountains on the wing of a cloud.

"It has been a year since you arrived here," the abbot said. "In that time two dozen have joined your ranks and yet you remain the most pious of all."

He nodded in response, saying nothing out loud.

"I want you to travel to the chapel where God blessed Andrew and Beth. Do you know why?"

He shook his head. "No, brother."

"You will know when you arrive."

It had rained for the entire duration of his journey. He had worn only the habit and it was soaked through, rubbing harshly on his skin as he slogged along mile after mile. His feet were bare, bleeding in places from the sharp stones he had encountered on the road. As time passed, he limped more and more, his hunger growing, gnawing at his insides.

He was glad of the pain, glad of the hunger, glad of the appalling weather. All those things tried his body but brought his soul closer to God, showing the Lord that he truly repented of his sins and could take any punishment that might be meted out.

For a month before he set out on his pilgrimage, his body had been troubled by a great ague. He had been in agony for days, his skin stretched thin, his insides churning and knotting over and over.

To be taken to the latrine, the brothers had to carry him on a sheet, his limbs rigid and unmoving.

He was still recovering when he set off, his limbs too weak to travel more than five miles a day. It took nearly a week to reach the castle and by the time he made it, he was almost dead on his feet.

They had been given notice of his arrival. He was admitted and Rory met him in the courtyard, bringing him into the chapel where Andrew and Beth were waiting, a baby laid asleep on the altar behind them.

"My laird," he said, prostrating himself on the cold tiles before him. "My lady," he added without looking up. "Forgive me, I beg you." Tears ran from his eyes, dripping onto the floor as he remained in place, refusing to stand, unable to shake the crushing guilt that threatened to consume him. That child was alive because he had failed. If he had succeeded in what he'd attempted to do, they would not be there, they would be in heaven, assured of their place by the Lord's side. Where would he be when his end came? The thought was terrifying. "Forgive me," he said again. "I am truly sorry for my crimes."

"Stand," Andrew said, holding an arm out toward him.

Derek took the offered hand, getting slowly to his feet, refusing to look the laird in the eye.

"How are you both?" he managed to ask, his toes curling under him.

"We are well and our bairn is well," Andrew said, stroking the forehead of the little one. "Our union was blessed."

""I prayed for you both."

"Thank you. And if I might ask of my father."

"The clans remain united and though he can be...difficult, he has an advisor who has made a difference to our parley."

Derek wondered who the advisor might be but thought better of asking. "He is well then."

"Aye, and our borders are strengthened. Gillis is over there now planning for his wedding and for possible English invasion."

"I will pray for him also."

Beth nodded. "Thank you." She paused, examining him closely. "We asked the abbot to send you here."

"If it is to punish me, so be it."

"We wish you to bless our child," Andrew replied. "Will you do as we bid?"

"Of course," Derek said, almost falling as he staggered forward. He leaned on the altar, looking down at the wee bairn wrapped in the purest white linen. "What name have you given your heir?"

"Janet," Beth said. "After my mother."

A wave of dizziness washed over Derek. He felt the truth of God's word take over him and it gave him strength. He stood tall, the ache in his limbs fading as he began the ceremony. "We ask you, our Lord, to give strength, faith, and love to this child today. May she prove herself worthy of all that you ask and may we be grateful for your grace and protection now and always."

"Amen," Andrew and Beth said in unison as Derek placed the tip of his forefinger on Janet's chest.

"Amen," he echoed.

The strength that had entered him ebbed away. Andrew squeezed him on the shoulder once before walking away. Beth did not follow at once. She looked at Derek closely. "You truly are sorry, aren't you?"

He nodded. "There is not a day that goes by that I do not regret what I did. I will take my guilt to the grave with me and beyond. Can I do anything else for you, my lady? Name it and it will be done."

"You like the chapel?"

"I think it is perfect."

"Then you may remain in it for as long as you wish. God forgive you, Derek."

She walked away then, leaving him to his thoughts. He was in awe of their ability to forgive. He had burned a hall, killing a number of the clan. He had personally brought down the ceiling of the chapel, killing more. They would have been perfectly within their rights to have had him executed and what did they do instead? They allowed him to bless their child.

It felt jarring to think of the person he used to be. He looked up at the ceiling, seeing it in all its glory. Was he the same person who had tried to bring that ceiling down on the heads of the laird and lady?

He knelt before the altar, giving thanks to God that he had been caught. He had a chance at salvation through repentance for his sins. He would not waste it.

The sun cast a light through the window, a break appearing in the clouds outside. A single shaft of golden glow struck the cross on the altar. Derek began to pray.

For many hours he begged for mercy. He had no idea how long he'd been there but it was dark when the door opened and they came in.

It wasn't Andrew and Beth, he knew that by the sound of their heavy feet. Two men, both strangers. He didn't look at them. He continued to pray as they talked loudly in the darkness.

"How do you know it was that doorway? " one asked. "The stones could have ended up anywhere."

"We're here now, aren't we?"

"I don't know. Are we? I can't see a thing in this goddamned darkness."

"Did you bring a flashlight?"

"I didn't know it would be night time, did I?"

"Christ, you're an idiot."

Derek was shocked by such casual blasphemy. "You are in a house of God," he said before he could stop himself. "Have some respect if you care for your souls."

"Look, there. What is he, a monk?"

"You, " said one of the voices, now addressing Derek. "What year is this?" He walked over and Derek caught a glimpse of the most bizarre clothing. It was like nothing he'd ever seen before.

"It is the year of our Lord 1191. Come, pray with me, brothers."

The sound of the door closing and then nothing. No sound other than the rain falling outside. Derek tried to resist temptation but he could not do it. He turned his head. There was no one there. He stood up and walked to the door, looking out into the darkness. No one there either. The only footprints in the moonlit mud were his own. Where had the blasphemers gone?

He looked back inside, glancing up at the vaulted ceiling that was barely visible in the gloom. "Are you testing me, Lord?" he asked out loud.

There was no answer spoken but he heard one nonetheless, returning to the altar and resuming his prayers. Whoever they were, they were nothing to do with him. Perhaps there had been no one at all. During the worst of the ague he had thought he'd heard many conversations, seen many things that could not possibly be there, figures floating past him in the darkness, demons crawling over his body, their tongues wrapping around his throat, choking him into oblivion. This was likely another vision, another test of his resolve. He had failed by becoming distracted from his prayers. He must be strong, he must concentrate on repentance, not on the worldly affairs of others.

"I pray you give strength to Beth and Andrew " he said out loud, his voice echoing around the chapel. "Bless their union, my Lord, I beg you."

*

Eight centuries later two men walked through a doorway into a brightly lit room. The noise of the traffic outside was jarring after the near silence of the chapel in the past.

"It's true," one said. "I can't believe it's really true."

The other man sank into a chair, shaking his head slowly. "What good does it do us if they aren't where they're supposed to be? We're going to have to tell him."

"He's not going to like it."

"No." A sigh as he dug a cellphone out of his pocket. "No, he is not."

The End

Also by the Same Author

Highlander's Voyage (Medieval Highlander Trilogy - Book 1)

A modern woman thrust back into the brutal past. A medieval highlander who lost everything dear to him. Why has fate brought these two broken souls together?

Carol Harper didn't want to travel through time. She only wanted to see if the ancient ring she found would fit on her finger. A single touch and she's back in the Middle Ages, held against her will by an enormous highlander and his army.

Angus MacClean is raiding with his fellow warriors when a strange woman appears out of nowhere. His clan believe witchcraft brought her into their midst but Angus has no fear of sorcery. Only one thing frightens him, the way his beautiful captive makes him feel.

To successfully evade the wicked English lord who hunts them both, they must put aside their burning desire. Fail and they risk capture by the cruellest of villains, a man who wants Angus dead and Carol all to himself.

Get your copy here

She's a damaged woman trapped in the past. He's a medieval highlander who's never known love. Until it lands in his lap.

When Fiona Carrington travels through time to 13th century Scotland she's no idea how to get home. All she knows is first she'll need to find a way out of the heavy chains wrapped around her body.

Kirk MacClean is trapped in a dungeon with no way out. When a mysterious woman appears out of nowhere he makes her a deal. He'll help her get back home if she helps him escape.

Working together, they might be able to win their freedom. But can they ignore their mutual attraction long enough to outrun the dark forces that threaten to destroy them both?

Get your copy here

True love is waiting for her back in twelfth century Scotland. If only she can find it.

When she was twelve, Alice met a boy she fell in love with. Then he vanished as if he'd never existed. Ten years later she finds a portrait of him in a museum dedicated to highland history. But how can the boy in the centuries old painting be the same boy she once met? Reaching out to touch the past she suddenly finds herself in the middle ages and in the middle of a clan war. In the distance is someone she recognizes. Someone very special.

Ramsey MacClean never expected to see Alice again. All his efforts have been focused on getting his lairdship back from the cruel usurper who snatched it from him. The last thing he needs is a distraction. But when a beautiful woman appears from nowhere his willpower starts to crumble. What's worse is it's the one woman he always swore to protect. Now he must choose between his clan and his desire. He knows he must let Alice go and concentrate on saving his people but the magic that brought her back has one final spell to cast, a spell that might just change the entire future of the highlands.

Get your copy here

Author's Note

Thank you for reading. If you enjoyed this book, please consider leaving a review on Amazon. An honest review of this book will help other readers choose their next book.

You can sign up for my newsletter at https://blanchedabney.com/sign-up/ to find out first when new books go live. You can also see some of the sights and sites that inspire me over on my Instagram page at www.instagram.com/blanchedabney.

I have tried to be as historically accurate as possible, using real names, places, and dates as much as is consistent with my research. Any mistakes made relating to the period are mine and mine alone and I am open to all feedback especially regarding historical accuracy for this and future stories. You can get in touch with comments, suggestions or corrections at:

contact@blanchedabney.com

Copyright